The Company of Strangers

THE
COMPANY
OF
STRANGERS

STORIES

JEN MICHALSKI

BRADDOCK
AVENUE
BOOKS
UNCOMMON BOOKS · UNCOMMON READERS

Some of these stories have appeared previously in *Barrelhouse* ("Your Second Left Fielder"), *Chicago Quarterly Review* ("Eat a Peach"), *The Cincinnati Review* ("The Club of the Missing"), *The Collagist* ("The Meteor"), *Frigg Magazine* ("The Company of Strangers"), *Fringe Magazine* ("The Piano"), *Grace in Darkness: Grace & Gravity, Vol. VIII* ("Great White"), *Lit Mag* ("After Life"), *The Literarian* ("The Goodbye Party"), *Little Fiction* ("The Loneliest Creature on Earth"), *The New Yinzer* ("The Bowling Story"), *Smokelong Quarterly* ("I'm Such a Slut and Don't Give a Fuck"), *Superstition Review* ("Are You Ready to Be Heartbroken?"), and *Tahoma Literary Review* ("Scheherazade").

Printed in the United States of America
10 9 8 7 6 5 4 3 2 1

ADVANCE REVIEW COPY, 2022

ISBN 10: 8-9857256-2-9
ISBN 13: 979-8-9857256-2-9

Book design by Savannah Adams

Braddock Avenue Books
P.O. Box 502
Braddock, PA 15104

www.braddockavenuebooks.com

Braddock Avenue Books is distributed by Small Press Distribution.

CONTENTS

THE COMPANY OF STRANGERS

STORIES

JEN MICHALSKI

AFTER LIFE

You were always more morose. In fact, you could never remember a time, exactly, when she complained about anything—her parents, her job, her friends. But she was delicate—in a way. There was a lack of permanence, a lack of tenaciousness, but still tough, like the way celery is impossible to break apart because of all those fibrous strands, and it never, ever rots, ever, even though you'd buy it and it'd sit in your shared refrigerator for months, waiting for you to begin your diet, because you were always the chubby one, always the sturdy, Eastern European dough girl, and she was the thin one, the one who people always asked whether she was dancer, a ballerina, a model. You were more like the celery, and she was not food at all, maybe rice paper, which is technically a food, although transparent and mostly lacking in nutritional value.

She was so nice. And that's what makes it so difficult for you to understand. Even when she broke up with you, she framed it in such a way that you didn't feel so bad, that she wasn't good enough for you, that you deserved better, that you should examine your options. And when you think about it, she was probably right, not because you are some great catch but because you never really knew her. You wondered if anyone ever did. You thought maybe she would let you in, that you would get to know her, but even at night, after you kissed her and ate her out and fisted her and licked her breasts and stroked her thighs, you asked her what she dreamed about, and it was always that she was in French club but realized she couldn't speak French or that she missed the ferry back from the Vineyard and got fired.

She had things. She went to all the camps, French and drama and some sort of Jewish religious camp with girls who went on to become psychologists or star in cable television comedies. You always went to parties with her, ones you wouldn't have normally been invited to because you were Polish and lower middle class and your mom signed you up for swimming lessons at the Y and the summer reading challenge at the library because there was nothing else to do in your neighborhood except get high behind the 7-Eleven and listen to hair metal bands. You'd stand by the serving spread and sample smoked trout on crackers the size of half dollars and she would be in the middle of the room, head arched back, laughing with someone she went to school with at Smith, her doubles partner from day school, god knows what she talked about and you thought these people didn't know her either, because they were so transparent but maybe she was, too, and when you complained about them on the ride back to the apartment she'd laugh and touch your thigh and say, "They're just friends. You're my girlfriend."

What privileges were bequeathed to you as girlfriend, you're not certain. You saw her without her makeup on, sure, but was it really a terrible secret that she read *Vanity Fair* on the toilet? That she ate almost nothing, that jar of Nutella that she'd spoon while watching the late-night talk shows, and cereal? That when she farted, she laughed in apology, and it was almost too cute? There was nothing, on the surface, to suggest anything terrible, and maybe that's why you found yourself looking through her desk, her computer, her purse, the trash, when she was on the phone or outside on the balcony, having her once-a-week cigarette. You were not looking for evidence of an affair, or bulimia, or membership to a terrorist cell, just *something*. You were looking for dirt that you could rub between your fingers, a grit that would catch under your fingernails, take days to scrub out. Something that would leave a mark.

She said you were too clingy, too questioning, too suspicious—not everyone had to be damaged, at least damaged in a way that rendered one non-functional. Not everyone had to be difficult or deep or mysterious. Not everyone had to be like you. But everyone had to be someone, you thought, and not like someone. Not a person only on paper, especially not rice paper. But she made you laugh, the silly songs she made up about the cat, or how her trip to the grocery store, uneventful for most, became the most-fucked-up-thing ever because she ran into that guy she used to do improv with when she graduated from college and he was buying vaginal cream for his girlfriend because she was too embarrassed and how he quizzed her on the finer points of the three-day versus the seven-day and there was that kid in the aisle with the mom who freaked out because colon cleanses made their way into the conversation. And then, she left her keys, somehow, in the produce section, right by the melons, and it took her an hour to find them, isn't that crazy, because neither of us eats fruit, right?

Sometimes when she'd sleep, you'd watch her, and deep in dream she would frown, or flinch, and you questioned her when she woke up but she said you were being paranoid, that she couldn't even remember what she was dreaming about. She would then ask about your dreams and you'd had a particularly disturbing one, how you sat with your dying grandmother and she smelled, she smelled so horribly of decay, and you'd known it'd been weeks since she showered, she could barely move, but she put her head on your shoulder, and you knew she missed being touched because no one ever touched her anymore, and it wasn't her fault, that she was so gnarled and foul-smelling and immobile, her eyes milky and weepy and you realized this woman was a child once, a girl, a woman who fucked, who loved and hated and regretted, and all she could do was put her head on her granddaughter's shoulder while her granddaughter tried not to breathe.

She was clever that way, always turning things back to you, like a psychiatrist, and maybe you were so fucked up yourself it took you a few years to catch on, to recognize this game of deflection and to call her out on it, and why didn't she dream, why wasn't she ever unhappy when you could see it sometimes, in the briefest of moments when she thought you weren't looking, the way she frowned and chewed her fingernails, then she'd freak out in the car on the way home from a birthday party because she thought she was mean to someone but she was never anything but nice to everyone, always complementing, always laughing, always caring, in such a way that no one ever thought she was fake, and if they did, they would never say it aloud because they'd look petty, a bitter sister, and it was that way, the way they felt for a minute, that you felt all the time, that she was a mirror that showed you all your faults and when you reached out for her it was your own hand coming back toward you, your own warts, your own insecurities.

You were thankful she stayed with you. It became easier—imperative—after a while, for your own sanity, to believe in her, believe she was happy, successful, beautiful—and she was beautiful and successful, of course—and that she would make you a better person by association. And you tried. You tried to iron that shit out—all your wrinkles, all your neuroses, your disappointments, your snark. You tried to be like her, but it felt like scooping everything out of yourself and tossing it into the laundry basket before you left the apartment. You felt nothing, and that didn't make you sad, so maybe that was good. But it didn't make you happy, either.

When she broke up with you, you took it badly. You blamed yourself. You could never rise to whatever level of Zen she had clung to. You were afraid of such heights. She said you'd changed, and when you pointed out that you had, that you tried so hard to be like her, she said she liked who you had been. But you weren't sure whether you had liked who she had been, because she'd never been anybody. And that wasn't the point, because she dumped you, and in that equation, the dumped is always at fault.

You moved to this new city, where you are now. It folded around you like your grandmother, and it was something you got used to. Its scents, its dirt. It was you. What you knew. But you stayed friends with her on Facebook, and she stayed in the old city, and had those friends, that cat. There was nothing to suggest she was unhappy or that she missed you. And no one told you that she did it, you just found out because of the Facebook posts people left on her page. Hundreds of them. In hysteria, in shock. But why she did it—no one ever asked you. If they thought you were the reason why she did it, you would never know. They never spoke to you after the breakup. It wasn't mean or spiteful; they just receded, like waves, back into their massive, glittery, transparent ocean in which you, of heft, of gravity, always flailed, always felt like you were drowning.

How could you live with her for so long—four years—and make her come, watch her sleep, buy groceries together, how could you not know she would do something like that? How could you not see she was unhappy? And if you were with her for so long, how could she not tell you? How could you not know someone at all? Why did you stop digging?

You are not responsible. You know this. But you lie awake at night and think about the dreams in which she had forgotten how to speak French, got stranded in the fucking Vineyard—would have been out of bounds to suggest she speak to someone, take something, go on a journey of self-discovery, on such flimsy evidence? And what did she want in you—did she want to live vicariously through your faults, your moods, your failures, her head on your shoulder, with her hair that smelled like Paul Mitchell, her breath that always smelled like gum?

There are things that you keep in your apartment in your new city—they were of no great importance to your relationship, exactly, just some things you have kept after your life with her. A CD she made you of French chanteuses that she gave you after your second date. A rubber bat she hung on the mirror of your car one Halloween morning. A necklace she always wore but never told you its origin—a broken crystal in a handmade wire setting. Had someone made it for her? Had she made it herself, in summer camp? You took it thinking she would contact you, ask you if you had stolen it, demand you give it back. It was important to her, and she could not live without it. She never did. You stopped wearing it after a few weeks because the crystal dug at your breastbone, left a little red welt. The little wire scraped your flesh. You tried to remember whether it had agitated her skin like it had yours. Had she never taken it off, even to shower, to sleep? Did she move it from one side to the other, trying to find where it irritated her the least? And if it bothered her so much, and how could it not, with its impossible craftsmanship, why didn't she take it off?

You thought about returning it after you found out what had happened, maybe sending it to her mother, her sister, even though you'd only met them once. She said she was on good terms with her family, adored them, but you never visited them, nor them you, and they never called, to your knowledge. You had always just assumed it was because they didn't like you. You still thought it should be returned to her, wherever it was she wound up—but those details were never offered to you. A few weeks after it happened, someone deleted her Facebook and her Instagram. Or you were deleted. Does it matter which one it was?

The necklace, at least, is still yours, although it never was. It's all you have and you can't get rid of it. Not because you want to keep it, but because everything needs a word, an answer. When your new girlfriend moves in, it hangs in your bedroom window. You never offer its origin. Most of the time it's just there, like a crack, a nick on the dresser, that you are aware of but somehow stop seeing. Although sometimes the sun catches the crystal, refracts the light, and spreads little rainbows on the wall. They are always changing their places. You never know, where things will be, from moment to moment.

THE LONELIEST
CREATURE ON EARTH

Thank you for humoring our son; he's a very inquisitive boy and knows a lot for his age. Other boys will astonish (or perhaps bore) you with their encyclopedic knowledge of Minecraft or Tyrannosaurus Rex but our son will tell you about Frank Hayes, the jockey who died of a heart attack mid-race at Belmont Park but still won because his body stayed in the saddle until man and horse crossed the finish line. I know you are about to visit your mother, but our son is not finished telling you about the whale who has been without a mate for over twenty years because his mating call is so different from other whales that no one responds to him.

"I bet he's the loneliest creature on earth." Our son widens his eyes as he speaks to you, and yes, your mother is waiting on the fifth floor, so thank you for lingering, telling him he's a smart boy, smiling just as widely as he is staring even though you feel sorry for him and maybe hug your own kids a little tighter or order the bloomin' onion loaf that they always whine for at the restaurant but that you never get, because of triglycerides and all, but now that you've seen our son you think hell, they'll only live once.

He's no idiot savant or anything like that; there's really quite a banal explanation for his repository of trivia. Last year at his annual health checkup one of us forgot to bring the tablet, the one with all the games on it, and, panicked, we went to the gift shop looking for a children's book and returned with a copy of *Weird and Amazing Facts.* It seemed harmless, with the blue monkey and red eyes on the cover. Our son became so engrossed he read it through his checkup¾the tongue depressor, the rubber reflex hammer to the knee, even the booster shot,.

We've since bought the full set—did you know there are eight? Our son has read them cover to cover, and while awaiting the publication of volume nine (yes, we checked the publisher's website), has memorized 287 weird facts. Like the reindeer that spent six weeks on the British submarine HMS Trident during World War II. Or Giethoorn, the village in the Netherlands with no roads, only canals and footbridges. Now when we are waiting for the doctor, he will entertain the other patients. At first, it made them less anxious of their own ailments, but after a while, they all began to sit on the other side of the waiting room. Not because of our son's retelling of the Fulgates of Troublesome Creek, a family in Kentucky who had blue skin from a rare genetic condition known as methemoglobinemia they had inbred into their family tree, but because they were worried about contagion.

We've been assured that this is not an issue. Anyway, we touch him all the time and are none the worse for wear. It's actually more dangerous for him than of us. Right after the checkup, we knew something wasn't right. We'd only grabbed his earlobe between our fingers and tugged at it playfully. They didn't believe us in the emergency department, called in child protective services, even accused us of devil worship. Why the hell would we cut it off, we explained over and over—we're telling you IT JUST CAME OFF. And when the tip of his pinky fell off, right there, in front of the child protective services woman and the nurse, only then did they believe us.

It sounds like one of those things in those books of his, people often say to each other. Never to us, although we know you're thinking it. Maybe you go home and Google search "body parts fall off" or "flipper for hand" or "purple-blue-green skin" and you finally learn that no, leprosy doesn't cause body parts to fall off but maybe our boy does have that methemoglob-blu-ey-oma thing. But that doesn't explain the red pupils and the sloughing, whole sheets of it, left behind on the examination table or in the pool (back when we went to places like that, back before the home schooling). And what a trooper he is, you add, to whoever it is you're talking to, your husband, your wife, your therapist, although we agree. He's an inspiration to us all.

That's not quite true. We're not inspired by what's happening; we're terrified. And when we're not terrified, we're angry. Especially when our little boy caught us crying in the bedroom a few months ago—we were holding his baby picture, when he was still himself¾and he proceeded to tell us that icebergs make a distinctive fizzing sound when they melt, called the *bergy seltzer*. Will you just be *quiet—quiet—quiet*—for once we shook him, didn't he have any idea how hard this was on all of us, and we felt our fingers sink into his skin, right to the bone, like we were squeezing gelatin. That scared us pretty bad. The holes absorbed after a few hours, and the fingerprints, which were—we kid you not, gold—faded after a few days.

The people from the government—one of those alphabet organizations¾came. Of course, they were careful, mindful of our stresses, talked about finding a cure, but we knew they just wanted to take him to some laboratory in some nondescript sandstone building in the DC suburbs and take blood samples, run tests. Try to culture something, but what—the rest of him? He's already lost, since the pinky, his whole left arm and his right foot. His skin, at one point a beautiful aquamarine blue (no filter) is now covered with scales and what appear to be short porcupine-like quills. At least there's no worry about sinking our hands into his skin anymore.

He doesn't seem fazed by these phases. He talks excitedly about the ninth volume of *Weird and Amazing Facts*, which should arrive any day now. Until then, he's fond of recounting the laughing epidemic, which is what he tells you when we run into you again, outside the elevators¾how is your mother, by the way? Who knows why we come here now, merely to document changes without any hope of answers. We're a little worried about the right kneecap—it was as wobbly as a wheel with loose lug nuts when we pulled on his sweatpants this morning. As you linger, smiling, trying not to stare at our son's bulbous knuckles as he waves his hands, he tells you that the laughing epidemic happened in Tanzania in 1962 and lasted a year. Thousands of people, in addition to laughing, couldn't stop crying, or fainting. They broke out in rashes and had severe pain.

"What was the cause of the epidemic?" You ask him. You hold your breath, not because you can't wait for the answer, but because of the smell. Like burned flesh but also, strangely, licorice, that wafts off our son.

"I don't know," he answers, and frowns, what passes as a frown, now that his lips have begun to curdle. "They never tell you that part."

You see, there are only facts in those eight volumes. Sometimes it's better to repeat what's known. Later, we will explain to you at your mother's wake, that the final month was the worst for our son. Not because of his incapacitation or the anti-contamination chamber, but because there simply weren't enough kind people like you to come and visit him. No one for him to tell, for instance, that the man who found the 5000-year-old corpse named the Iceman in 1991 also was found frozen dead in ice in 1994. And goodness knows, we stopped listening to him months ago. We've had our own set of facts to try and get straight. What to tell our friends, our coworkers, our insurance agent, about what happened. How one day we woke up and got ready to feed him (such a strange process, really, at the end¾we had to put the nutrient drink in a spray bottle and mist it onto his skin) and when we opened the chamber, he was gone. In his place only what looked like a snakeskin skeleton and one red eyeball. It was the day the ninth volume of *Weird and Amazing Facts* came in the mail—we were so heartbroken he never got to read it.

Now, this is the weird thing. We tried to keep all of this under wraps—and unless somebody at the hospital said something—but where would they have gotten that picture? It was only stored on our phone. We never shared it on Facebook and save nothing to the Cloud. And yet there it was, on the cover of volume nine—that picture of him, his beautiful little boy face. Right before the checkup, the waiting room, the forgotten tablet, the book. Under the picture reads simply his name, Jeremy, what we know for sure.

THE LONG HAUL

I'm wondering why I even bought him the slippers—extra wide, tan suede, memory foam, brand name Old Man Romeo, for the ridiculous price of $29.95 at Wal-Mart of all places. It's never below 40 degrees in Arizona, and right now, standing on his doorstep at four in the afternoon, it's a sauna-like 94. But it's my Uncle Tony, and the last time I saw him, he was standing in our carport barefoot smoking a Marlboro, the lights from the police cars throbbing and shimmering in our driveway like a disco. His heels were bloody, his toenails, long and thick and some black. And I thought, even though I was only ten, that a man should take better care of his feet.

I survey the cul-de-sac of aluminum-siding double-wides as I knock. Where I stand, a silver Honda scooter rests in the driveway and an orange tomcat the size of a carry-on luggage lounges on the porch mat. Behind me, a voice booms like a PA system from a minor-league hockey game.

"Who the hell are you?"

I turn around and there he is at the end of the sidewalk by my rental car, wearing a track suit, sunglasses, and slide sandals like he's in the witness-protection program.

"It's me, Raymond," I say, holding up the box as an offering but also protection. "I brought you some slippers."

And just like that, we're sitting on the deck behind the house drinking Michelob, Uncle Tony thundering in and out of the sliding door with offerings.

"You gotta be hungry—they don't feed you nothing on the plane these days." He drops a party-size bag of Lays potato chips on the weather-beaten plastic deck table. "You want a sandwich? I got salami and cheese, some mustard. How 'bout just cheese, just like when you was little? I got one of those grills—George Foreman—I cook everything on that, my chicken, my steaks. My veggies."

He pauses during this avalanche of words to slap me on my back. "Jesus, Ray, twenty years! You ain't come out here to tell me your mother died, have you?"

"No." I sip the Michelob. My therapist said I didn't have to bring up anything if I didn't want. But then, why else come?

"I, uh, had this work thing up in Phoenix¾stylist conference."

"What?" Tony raises his eyebrows. "Like hairdressers or something?"

"Exactly." I nod. "Anyway, Aunt Debbie said you'd settled out here, so I thought I'd come see you."

"Debbie," Tony laughs like it's the funniest thing that's ever been said. "Thank God she's a goddamn busybody, huh? Bless her heart, she's the only one who still talks to me. I never thought you ever would."

He stares at me, grinning. There was a time when I thought Uncle Tony was handsome, but it was a time when I didn't know much. When I was young, he reminded me of John Travolta when he was in *Grease*; now, he looks and sounds more like an old Andrew Dice Clay—wide cheeks, small forehead but with a big, silvery pompadour to even out the proportions.

"Well, you look very fancy—very dapper." Tony inhales quickly, still smiling, and I watch him take in my skin-tight button-up Oxford, slim-cut lavender shorts, and Sperry top-siders.

"It's hot out here." I look away, pushing up my shirt sleeves.

"You don't like this weather?" He does a panoramic of the backyard with his hand, as if this somehow makes his point, but all I see is a bunch of double-wides bunched together, all with beaten-down lawn furniture, snaky hoses in brown grass, bug lights. "When I'm home, this is my little slice of heaven. I'm glad you caught me—I'm taking a load out to Connecticut on Thursday."

Tony's sister, that goddamn busybody Debbie—told me that he's been a long-haul trucker for years; maybe that's why it was easy for me to make this side trip. There was a good chance he wouldn't be home, and I could feel good about trying.

"So try on your slippers." I nudge the box, resting on the table, toward him. "I got a receipt."

"A receipt—you don't know how special this is to me." He lowers himself gingerly in the plastic deck chair—more for the chair's sake, I suspect, than his own. "I ain't gotten a present from nobody for a long time."

"Not even your lady friends?" I joke. I know, as soon as it comes out of my mouth, it's the wrong thing to say, and just as quickly, I'm bent over my Michelob, peeling at the label.

We sit in silence for a moment before I hear the rustle of tissue paper. When I look up, he's angling one of the suede slippers over a corn on his big toe.

"If they're too small..." I start.

"They're perfect." He's standing up, admiring them as I press the cold bottle to my face. "I've never had a more perfect present."

* * *

When I was ten, when Tony was in-between jobs, he babysat me and my nine-year-old sister, Joelle, on the nights our mom worked at the Sky-High Cocktail Bar. Two or three evenings a week, Tony would arrive at 6:00 and, if my mother hadn't placated us with bowls of cereal or leftover pizza, Tony would pull out the frying pan and whip up scrambled eggs or grilled cheese sandwiches.

"Did you do your homework?" He cooked with a cigarette tucked behind his ear and a can of Coors in his left hand and whisper-sang Van Halen songs with sexual innuendos that completely eclipsed mine and Joelle's comprehension. Then we'd pile onto the couch and watch *Melrose Place*, Tony's favorite show.

"That Kimberley, she's one calculating bitch." Tony shook his head as she plotted Michael's death with the flighty and impulsive Sydney. "I wouldn't kick her out of bed, though."

"I kicked Raymond out of bed once." Joelle nodded sympathetically. "But that's because he farts a lot."

"Shut up, you lying bitch." I grabbed a handful of Joelle's hair, the color of a penny, and pulled.

"Hey." Tony reached around Joelle, who was nestled in his armpit, to whack me on the side of the head. "Language. Jesus, where do you learn that shit? School?"

Tony was a punctual and adequate minder, a perfect complement to our lower middle-class childhood of copious television, lack of vegetables, and secondhand cigarette smoke. I couldn't imagine evenings without his volcanic perspiration,

Drakkar Noir cologne, his encyclopedic knowledge about grades of gold jewelry, and his interest in ensembles of young, single people on network television. And, like most young, self-absorbed children, I imagined we were Tony's world.

***

"Sorry I'm late." Tony stepped into the doorway one afternoon, I, still holding the phone trying to reach my mom at work to tell her Tony had gone missing. Behind him, like a magic trick, stood a woman. "I had to pick Veronica up at work."

"Hi." She wore a fringed jean jacket and white boots, her hair so traumatized by styling the ends split like tulips. She looked at us from the porch the way my mom did the women with religious pamphlets who often showed up Saturday mornings on our doorstep. "I'm Tony's friend."

"These are the kids." Tony rubbed my head like a dog. "Well, Darlene's kids. But we're like a family, right?"

"Uncle Tony, I'm starving." Joelle picked her nose in an attempt to distract, I guessed, from her hunger.

"You said you were going to take me to Secrets." Veronica frowned at Tony.

"You gotta work tonight." Tony unhooked Joelle's little coat with the unicorn on the back off its hanger near the door. "Ray, put your boots on. We're going out to eat."

Twenty minutes later, Joelle and I sat across from Tony and Veronica at Denny's, studying laminated menus as Veronica dug out her beaded cigarette holder.

"Why didn't we go to a place that served drinks at least?" Veronica had not stopped frowning since we piled into Tony's Trans Am and fish-tailed across the icy February streets here.

"Veronica is my girlfriend." Tony draped his arm over her shoulder. Her eyes wandered toward the ceiling. "One day, you two are going to have some cousins to play with."

"Won't we be too old then?" I questioned. Even then, I was a stickler for critical thinking.

"I want the spaghetti and meatballs." Veronica pushed her menu to the edge of the table and scooted out of the booth. "And a ginger ale. I'm gonna go smoke."

"We've been going together for a month or so." Tony rubbed a patch of stubble on his chin after she'd left. "I think she's the one."

"The one what?" Joelle worked furiously on the paper placemat with a green crayon. "And where do you go?"

"He loves her, stupid." I picked up my own crayon, blue, and drew a box, reinforcing the sides, making them thicker and thicker until just a blue box remained.

"Give me back my scarf." Joelle tugged at the purple chiffon scarf around my neck.

"Why are you wearing a scarf, anyway, sport?" Tony sipped at his water. I glanced outside the restaurant, where Veronica leaned on the hood of a car that wasn't Tony's, talking to a guy in a leather jacket.

"The guys in RATT wear scarves," I say after a beat. MTV's Headbanger's Ball was something that Joelle and I watched on the weekends, mostly because our other babysitter, Aunt Debbie, fell asleep on the couch with it on. We weren't fans of the music, but the amalgamation of leather and spandex and chiffon into a single outfit opened doors in my mind that I didn't know existed.

"On their heads, maybe." Tony scrunched his eyebrows, glancing out the window. His face set like cement. "Who the hell is that guy with Veronica?"

* * *

"Best steak in the desert, was I right?" Tony has pushed the passenger seat in my rental Hyundai all the way back. He holds a cigarette in his hand, ready to light it up the second I pull in his driveway. "All the big-wigs—the politicians and football players—go there."

"You really shouldn't have." The waist of my already-snug shorts digs into my guts as I cut the ignition. "At least let me buy breakfast tomorrow."

"As long as you're here, you're not paying for a thing." Tony waves me off. "I ain't got nobody I'm spending money on."

"Nothing wrong with spending it on yourself." Outside the car in the darkness, the heat feels ominous, like a heavy breath on my neck. Down the street, a screen door creaks open.

"I'm just waiting to die, Ray." His cigarette glows alive in his mouth. "Might as well spend it all before I go."

Tony exhales, looking into the night, the bruised sky and small, faint moon. Suddenly he calls and whistles "Gizmo!" and the orange tabby runs up the porch steps with a speed that belies its size.

"I never took you for a cat person," I say as Tony unlocks the door.

"Yeah?" He grins, cigarette dangling out of his mouth. "Check this out."

In the living room he lumbers over to an ancient cabinet stereo and picks up a framed photo, holding it out to me. In it, Tony is sitting next to Santa Claus, Gizmo on Santa's lap.

"I got this done at the PetSmart. Gizmo is my family. Except you." He looks at me. He picks up another frame, in it my school picture from third grade, the last picture he has of me. But I reach for another—one of Joelle in second grade. Her teeth are too big for her soft, freckled face, her eyes wide and brown. In her hair is a white plastic barrette with a duck on it.

"You're my only family, too, really." I put Joelle's photo back.

"You don't talk to your mother anymore?"

"We had some differences in worldview." I shrug. "So she stopped talking to me."

"Why, because you're a faggot?" Tony holds up my photo as if proof. "I'm sorry—I'm mean homosexual?"

"She was never the same after everything that happened." I look for Gizmo. I want something to hug. "I guess I couldn't be the person she needed me to me."

"None of that was your fault, though—it was mine." Tony puts the photo back on the stereo and picks up his new slippers, which sit by the door next to his black Caterpillar boots. "What are you drinking? You like vodka?"

"It's like ninety degrees out." I watch Tony slip on the Old Man Romeos. "You'll sweat right through those."

"There's a breeze outside. You like vodka cranberry?"

"Vodka tonic's fine." I rub the back of my moist neck and watch Tony rummage through the fridge from the doorway of the kitchen.

"How about a vodka lemonade?" He's holding a lime, a container of lemonade-flavor Crystal Light, and, inexplicitly, a jar of salsa.

"Does it bother you, the gay part?" I ask as he picks things up around the dark kitchen like he's preparing to evacuate for a hurricane. "We don't all drink fruity cocktails."

"You don't?" He stops and looks at me. "I love 'em. The drinks I mean—not the gays. I mean, the gays are all right."

"Just all right?"

"Let me tell you something." He puts a lime on the cutting board and pulls a knife out of the drawer. "All them showers at the rest stops for truckers—they're full of guys looking to stick their dick in something or the other way around. Someone was telling me that, in the Middle East, men have sex with each other all the time when they're ain't no women around, and nobody considers themselves gay."

Before I can respond, he waves the knife in the air to make a point: "You know what I do when I'm at the rest stops, Ray? Not looking for no guys. I'm not even looking for women. I'm looking for Joelle."

***

"She's cheating on me, I know it." Tony lit a cigarette by the frying pan as Joelle's cheese sandwich sizzled. "I called her apartment twice but her roommate says she's taking a nap."

"Why couldn't she be taking a nap?" I sat at the table in my mother's bathrobe. Although I claimed to feel under the weather, mostly I just like the color—rose—and the feel of the chenille on my arms and back. "We take naps all the time."

"Adults don't take naps." Tony took several drags of the cigarette in succession. "She's lying to me—I bet she's at the CatCall right now dancing for Mr. Monte Carlo."

"That's his name?" Joelle asks from the doorway. "Is my grilled cheese burning?"

"No." Tony's tone was mocking. "That's not his name, that's the name of his car. Shit—yes, your grilled cheese is burning."

He slid the spatula into the smoky pan and retrieved Joelle's sandwich, black on one side.

"If I could just go over there and prove it." Pinching the sandwich between his fingers, he dropped it into our trash can. "But she knows I'm here babysitting, so she's gold, you know?"

"We could go with you, Uncle Tony." I offered. "We could just sit in the car."

"I can't let you do that." Tony shook his head. "I don't know what's going to happen if I find her in there with Mr. Monte Carlo."

"You could take us to McDonald's and we can eat in the car," Joelle argued. "I can bring my Nancy Drew book in case I get bored. You ruined my grilled cheese—you owe me."

"Your argument is sound." Now he nodded. "But your mother would never forgive me if I let anything happen to you two. Plus, you'll get grease and crap all over my seats."

"We're not kids anymore." I stood up and disrobed, showing the scrawny chest of a 10-year-old. "We can sit in the car and eat McDonald's like adults."

Tony rubbed his temples so hard I thought they might catch on fire, like Joelle's cheese sandwich. Then he clenched his fists like a superhero doing epic battle with the villain in his brain. He took off my mom's apron and hung neatly it by the cupboard door.

***

"Do not leave this car." Tony mashed his cigarette into the ashtray. "Put all your wrappers in the McDonald's bag and hold it in your lap—do not let it touch the car, okay?"

From the backseat Joelle spread a napkin on her lap and set about opening her Happy Meal.

"If something happens, just keep honking the horn until I come out." Tony stood beside the passenger door now. He took a few deep breaths, shook out his arms, and walked into the concrete bar with a pink awning. In the window, a neon cat simulated a meowing sound. The windows themselves were tinted dark.

"That doesn't look like the bar mom works at," Joelle said from the back seat.

She was right. Although, in retrospect, I wouldn't call the Sky-High Cocktail Bar classy, it wasn't this place. Mostly men seemed to go inside, albeit a few women in fake furs and high heels.

"Eat your cheeseburger," I said, dipping a chicken nugget into my barbecue sauce.

"Raymond, what does 'titian' mean?" Joelle asked ten minutes later.

"I don't know—use it in a sentence."

"*Nancy, an attractive titian blond, grinned up at her friend.*"

"Oh, Nancy Drew." I sipped my drink. "I don't know, steely?"

"Why would she have hair like steel?"

"Can't you just look it up in the dictionary when you get home?"

Joelle was silent for another ten minutes, during which time I pondered asking her to read her book to me, I was so bored, but Joelle was a laborious reader with a lot of non-sequiturs pondered aloud, so I didn't.

"Ray, I have to pee."

"You can hold it."

"No, I can't. And Uncle Tony said not to get anything on the seats."

"Jesus, you're so annoying." I looked out the window, spotting a bush at the end of the building. I didn't want to leave the Trans-Am, since Tony took the keys. But I could see her safely from the car. "You're going to have to go in that bush."

"I can't." Joelle sounded like she was going to cry as I opened the door and slid out, pulling up the seat. "I can't go out in public like you can. I don't have a wee-wee."

"You're going to go in that bush, or you're going to hold it until you get home." I stared at her. "And throw away our trash in that can while you're over there."

Joelle climbed out carefully, squeezing her legs together as she stood. Then she wiggled across the asphalt toward the bush. I picked up her Nancy Drew book from where it lay opened, face down, on the back seat and flipped through the pages, looking for the black and white illustrations.

The door of the bar swung open, and Tony appeared, locked in a man sandwich. One man with a leather vest and handkerchief knotted over his head pulled at Tony's left arm, and another man behind me gripped him by the shoulders, pushing him forward.

"I wasn't doing nothing—she's the one cheating on me!" Tony dug his new black boots into the concrete, hunching over as the men tried to dislodge him from the doorway.

"I told you a thousand times, you can't touch the dancers," handkerchief man sad.

"She wasn't working!"

"Doesn't matter." Handkerchief man pulled at Tony's arm so hard I was afraid he was going to pop it out of its socket, but Tony wouldn't budge. I wasn't quite sure of his plan, but it looked like it involved flipping the man behind him over his shoulder like Chuck Norris. Just then, handkerchief man bent low and punched Tony in the stomach. I tossed Joelle's book in the car and joined the scrum, hitting handkerchief man in the ass with my fist.

"Don't hurt my uncle!" I screamed, and both men let go at once as if they'd been tasered.

"Get in the car, Ray." Tony dusted off the shoulders of his jacket as the men pondered their legal liability considering the young witness before them. "This place hires a bunch of two-timing whores."

"Don't ever come back here," handkerchief man warned. "Or you'll have more than a tummy ache next time."

"Get in the car, Ray—what did I tell you?" Tony's face was red and sweaty, and he walked a little hunched over.

"Joelle had to pee," I explained, glancing toward the bush. "Joelle, come on."

But there was no one crouched behind the bush. I ran over to the side of the building, ready to give her shit for wandering around, picking up interesting rocks whatever crap she always found on the ground, but she wasn't there, either.

"I don't know where she went," I choked up the words, my body feeling like it was turning inside out, as Tony staggered up.

"What the fuck did I tell you, Ray?" Tony pushed me into the side of the building. "About staying in the car?"

* * *

"She's gone." In the kitchen I put my hand on Tony's shoulder, giving his knife hand a wide berth. "She's dead."

"You don't know that." He turns back to the counter, slicing up a lime with a dexterity I didn't think he had in him. "I watch these shows all the time when I'm home—*Crime Stoppers* and stuff—you don't know all the girls who get taken for sex trafficking."

I remember the police arriving at the CatCall, Tony erupting when they told us we couldn't file a missing person's report until someone had been missing for more than 24 hours. I also remember him getting into a fight with Veronica, who'd come outside the bar at some point to see what all the excitement was, which ended in him spitting on her and us peeling out, only for the police to show up again at our house hours later to arrest Tony for assault. It's one of the last images I have of Tony, standing in our carport barefoot, his feet rubbed raw from walking for miles in his new boots around town, looking for Joelle. Actually, it *is* the last image I have of him, since Mom banned him from the house, from seeing us ever again.

"I don't think she's alive anymore." I sit at the deck table. "As much as I want her to be, in my gut, I just don't think she is."

"The bodies they found, they didn't match her dental records." Tony lights a cigarette as he paces on the deck. "I'm on the road forty weeks out of the year. I go places, I see people, talk to people—I ain't never stopped looking."

I close my eyes. Sometimes, often, I imagine what Joelle would look like now—what her voice would sound like, what she would've majored in, assuming she went to college (her grades weren't great, but I also thought she needed glasses, something I'd been bugging our mom about in the months before she went missing). I wonder about the man who took her, what he was thinking. If he's alive. The police interviewed everyone at the bar again and again, poured over scant spotty video camera footage from the gas station across the street, even the cold case detectives years later. How does a girl walk to a bush to pee and then disappear?

"Sometimes I just stand outside the restroom at the welcome centers, and I shout 'Joelle!' just to see if anybody looks up." Tony's glass is close to his lips, his eyes watery.

"Does anyone ever look up?" I feel my eyes water too, tell myself it's the generous pour of the vodka.

"So why did you come?" Tony asks, frowning. Not in suspicion, but sadness.

"I don't know—to see how you were." I shrug. Since I was thirteen, right after I took a bunch of my mom's Nembutals and had to have my stomach pumped at the hospital, I never thought about Tony, ever. Or Joelle, if I could help it. I never thought about anything. The same way Joelle disappeared, Raymond did, too, and Ray appeared in his place, a flamboyant, happy-go-lucky BA-in-commercial arts-turned-stylist. A stylist attending the Salon & Spa Expo conference in Phoenix, who happened to tell his Aunt Debbie, who happened to mention the conference's proximity to Tony. A stylist who watched Raymond, Joelle, and Tony spill out of his body, like an emptied bag of marbles. Who was having trouble putting them all back in.

"I just hope you ain't never blamed yourself. I should've never taken you two to the CatCall." Tony coughs for like five seconds and pats his thigh for Gizmo, who's looking at him in alarm from the corner of the deck. "Don't worry—daddy ain't going to kick yet."

"I don't." I pick up the Stoli bottle and aim for my glass, splash the table a little. "I don't blamed you, either."

This wasn't always true. And maybe it wasn't entirely true when I drove up to the house this afternoon. But now, I don't know. I've blamed myself, Tony, my mother, the monster who took Joelle. But blame is a completely useless verb, noun, whatever. It doesn't change the past or the future. And yet the deck is stacked with them, sometimes the only cards.

"That's nice of you to say." Tears run like boulders down Tony's cheeks as he encases Gizmo's head with his hand. "It makes me feel like there's something to live for—you and Joelle."

"You should try to go on with your life." I hold the vodka glass with both hands, the perspiration from the glass dripping in my palms.

"How?" Tony rolls Gizmo up his leg and onto his lap. "I can't date—once you start to get serious, how do you tell someone you lost your niece outside a titty bar?"

I think of the men at bars with whom I've gone home, always going to their place to have sex, giving them a fake number the morning after. The thought of bringing up Joelle with anyone is like resuscitating the dead, to have that zombie following you around again. Not that the zombie ever leaves you. But for years I've been a zombie, too, because they don't feed on their own.

When I decided to see Tony, though, I packed Joelle's Nancy Drew book and, on the flight here, I opened it and read the word titian over and over and willed myself to be steely.

"Why don't you come on the next haul with me?" Tony says after a minute. "It'd be nice to catch up for real. We don't have to talk about all that stuff, you know. Just something."

"To Connecticut?" I laugh. "You snore like a power washer."

"I got one of those CPAP thingies now," he says. "Anyway, I could just drop you home, on the way. Save you a flight back."

"I already paid for the ticket," I answer, as if I'm considering it. There is so much I could tell him that I haven't told anyone else, and him me. But feelings—they're so much like blame—another useless verb, noun whatever.

"Well, I just thinking aloud—spit-ballin'." He crushes his empty box of Newports. "I gotta get more cigarettes. Can you drive me to the 7-Eleven?"

"I can't." I feel unsteady just sitting in the chair. "How about the scooter?"

"You serious?" Tony laughs, heavy and wet. "You wanna drive that?"

"I want to ride on the back, I think." I put my palms on the table and slowly unfold myself to a standing position. "It goes like thirty, tops, right?"

***

Thirty miles per hour in the open air without a helmet feels like ninety in the closed cabin of a car. I press my bare head against the top of Tony's back, to keep out of the stinging wind, and think about the stack of flyers I noticed in his living room before we left: MISSING: JOELLE ESPOSITO printed atop, her photo underneath. It'd been xeroxed so many times she was an inkblot of a girl. A girl who could be anyone, nowhere and everywhere at once.

At the 7-Eleven I stand outside and wait, the heat so thick it's pressing me into place. Inside Tony jerks his head back, laughing at something the cashier says. I study his profile, think of what I could do with his hair, shaving the temples close but keeping his sideburns, losing the pompadour. I imagine us in Tony's rig, driving through Las Cruces, El Paso, Dallas, and we are moving away and toward things.

I hear the jingle of the door as I bend over the trashcan, throwing up all the marbles.

"Christ, Raymond, you okay?" I feel Tony's hands on my shoulders.

I shake my head. Tears burn my cheeks as I mouth the word titian over and over, into stench of my own vomit, willing myself to be steely.

THE METEOR

The meteor fell from the sky and landed in the couple's yard. It charred the grass and flattened the grill and sent the soccer ball whining until it was flaccid. It pulsed, a white and orange marbled planet, stoic, propelling waves of heat through the neighborhood, wilting the tulips next door, melting the tires of a Toyota RAV4. The woman came out of the house, drawn to the murmurous sphere, to the undulating marble lava moving in its core. She walked across the warm soot, embers stinging her face, the waves becoming hotter and hotter. The man came out of the house.

We have to leave. He pulled at her synthetic shirt, which had begun to melt to her skin. *The whole neighborhood has to evacuate.*

I want to stay. She did not look at him. *I think I am in love.*

With the meteor? He squinted his eyes at the white-hot light, pulling at her arms. *Are you crazy?*

Don't you feel the enveloping warmth of its heart? She struggled to free herself from his grasp. *Don't you understand the radiance of its mind?*

It's going to kill you. He hooked her by the arms and began to drag her away. *You'll thank me later.*

The fire department came. Fire trucks from several municipalities joined in, and the firemen knocked down fences and sawed down trees until they could surround the burning rock with their hoses. They sprayed the water, and steam filled the air, burning the neighborhood squirrels and raccoons. The powerful streams of water bounced off the meteor and pelted the aluminum siding of the houses, stripped paint off the cars.

Several times, particularly in the thick steam, the woman escaped the man and secretly made her way back to the meteor. The entire neighborhood waited in the gymnasium of the nearby high school except for the emergency response units and the man and the woman, who, without protective clothing, were badly burned. The woman was blind in one eye, and began to lose sight in the other, but with her arms in front of her, she felt her way again and again to the now-cooling mass.

Several hours later the meteor was the temperature of bath water. The neighborhood was ruined. The man urged the woman to go to the hospital.

I'll wear my scars as proof of my love. She stood on the warped frame of their patio door. The attached deck had long since burned away, and she looked strange, up there in space.

Weeks later, the community association met again in the gymnasium. They decided to move the meteor to a vacant field outside the neighborhood, behind a billboard that advertised DNA testing. Not because it was radioactive, or because it might disintegrate and leech into the drinking water, but because no one wanted to look at it, particularly the next-door neighbors, who could not bear the reminders of tragic events nor the damage they created to surrounding property values.

Everyone voted in favor except for the woman, who wanted the meteor to remain in their yard.

My love for the meteor will never die, she insisted. When it came time for the meteor to be removed, she appeared in the back yard wearing a black dress and watched from behind oversized dark sunglasses as the men rolled and coaxed its mammoth girth onto the bed of the tow truck, one they'd rented after a taking up a collection in the neighborhood.

The man forgave the woman. After all, the meteor landed in their yard, without provocation. In its own way, he supposed, it could be considered beautiful and pure. The chances of another meteor falling in their yard were incredibly remote. As she lay in bed recuperating from her injuries, he knew she would come to her senses, see the damage the meteor had caused.

Things got better. The man brought the woman chicken soup and diet 7-Up. They watched movies on Netflix in bed. Eventually the woman got well enough that she could sit on the couch, and they watched Netflix there. Sometimes they even held hands. It rained in the spring and the earth absorbed those tears. The dirt expanded and filled the depression of the meteor. Grass grew over it. The neighborhood slowly recovered. Squirrels ran along the newly constructed fences. Other things returned.

When the woman became well enough to leave the house, the man asked her where she wanted to go.

To the meteor, she answered. And she left.

The man brought chicken soup and Diet 7Up to the field behind the billboard, but the woman refused them. She sat and leaned against the hard, gray orb, trying to wrap her arms around it. At night, the man brought blankets to keep her warm, and a parka when it began to snow. Still, the woman grew thin. Her hair got matted. She looked homeless. The man could not understand why the woman he loved did not love him, was killing herself for a meteor.

He filed for divorce. The woman did not return, and he stopped visiting her. He heard that maybe she had taken ill, or died, but he kept himself from checking. He stayed in the house. After an extensive interview process, a new woman came to live with him. She seemed to have no interest in meteors or any other types of heavenly bodies. They watched Netflix on the couch. Things returned to normal.

One night a few years later, another meteor fell from the sky and landed in the yard of the couple. It charred the grass and flattened the grill and sent the soccer ball whining until it was flaccid. It pulsed, a white and orange marbled planet, stoic, propelling waves of heat through the neighborhood, wilting the tulips next door, melting the tires of a Toyota Prius. The man came out of the house, drawn to the murmurous sphere, its undulating marble lava moving in its core. He walked across the warm soot, embers stinging his face, the waves becoming hotter and hotter. The new woman came out of the house.

We have to leave. She pulled at his synthetic shirt, which had begun to melt. *The whole neighborhood has to evacuate.*

I want to stay. He did not look at her.

YOUR SECOND LEFT FIELDER

Your second left fielder, Denise, was retarded. But only you kids would say that, and only then, because it was the 1980s. She would be thirty-eight now, Denise, and her brother, Tommy, would insist that she be called developmentally delayed, or maybe he wouldn't because she was done developing, physically and possibly mentally. You wonder whether Denise is a virgin. When you worked at the center for developmentally disabled adults during college, sometimes your clients would grab at their privates, rub them like they were rubbing transfers onto paper, like dogs scratching their flanks. You had to distract them with their favorite blocks or bright plume feathers or Pound Puppy toys but few fell for it, and you waited uncomfortably until they were finished, and then you rubbed their hands down with soap and gel sanitizer. The masturbation made them more human, though. They couldn't speak, only grunt and cry, and many couldn't walk, strapped instead to modified wheelchairs on rolling beds. Outliers in so many other areas of their lives, their insatiable drive for sexual pleasure, even as if interfered with class time, meals, and the afternoon showing of *Runaway Bride* on DVD, placed them squarely in the middle of humanity's bell curve.

Let's be clear: this story isn't about Denise. She is a peripheral character. Perhaps everyone is, and that would make you protagonist. But what has changed, what challenge are you facing, really, except that you saw Dickey Richards, the pitcher on your co-ed little league team, the 1982 Eastwood Orioles, at the Exxon station? You know it was him because even though his ivory-yellow hair is now buttered sandstone and his hairline resembles the continent of Africa, his birthmark (shaped like a dolphin, you think) still stands in stark relief through the bristles of beard on the side of his neck.

It does not surprise you that he still lives here, in the town where you visit your parents, with the outdated split-levels lining cul-de-sacs that are slowly being surrounded by ethnic food restaurants and tat stores. But you wonder what would have happened if he knew you had a crush on him, all the way until ninth grade, before the soft taffy of his face and limbs stretched into hard, angular bends, before he became more praying mantis than man, before James Hilliard asked you to the prom? The same James Hilliard who you later lost your virginity to in the bathroom of the Super 8 while your classmates drank and listed to Snoop Dog just on the other side of the door.

As an adult, you always thought you would date someone who liked Tom Waits. So much so that you never listened to Tom Waits, figuring your eventual lover would fill you in on his essential gems, the throwaways, the trivia that would give you street cred at hipster bars you frequented. Instead, you had to start by yourself, album by album. You like *Rain Dogs* okay but fell in love with *The Heart of Saturday Night* and what to make of *Blood Money*? But you have always been like this. You played little league because your brother did, and although you thought Jim Palmer was the cutest player, you traded all your good cards for Thurman Munson because Dickey thought Jim was the fairy in the underwear ads. Now you couldn't name one active baseball player except for Derek Jeter, and that's just as bad as having a crush on Jim Palmer.

You were better than a lot of the boys on the team, though. There was a boy, Frances, who sat on his glove in right field. And Bobby, who one game simply wandered from left field to the hot dog stand in the bottom of the fifth. The outfield was for the no-talents; there were actually four outfielders out there, if you included Denise, who was positioned so close to the left field foul line a mosquito couldn't slip between her and the chalk. You played second and even started one game as pitcher before getting pulled in the fourth after your pitches kept bouncing on home plate. You were a whiz at second, though, except for the game in which the batter, after threading the ball into left-center alley, tried to stretch a single into a double. Miraculously, Bobby got the ball back into the infield well before the hitter made it to second base. But you didn't realize the play was not a force, that you needed to tag the batter, and the batter was safe, much to the chagrin of Dickey, who was pitching a no-hitter at the time. The second-base umpire, a thirteen-year-old boy named Arnold, tried to explain the rules to you in-between pitches for the rest of the season, even consoling you that Dickey's no-hitter was broken up by the batter's single, not you, but you always ignored him, still sour about the botched tag.

Arnold, with his fro and wart-covered knuckle, was the guy you probably should have dated, rather than pining for guys like Dickey. Everyone loves the flashy pitchers, but the men behind the scenes, who kept the order and got none of the glory, were the grease that made the machine run smoothly. Or someone like Tommy, so fiercely protective of Denise, even if he looked the same at eleven as you imagined him looking now, gaunt with high cheekbones and sandy hair, a poor man's Gary Cooper or maybe one of those men in the Depression-era Walker Evans photos.

Guys like Joe, the groom of the bride whose wedding you are in town for, a college classmate you do not like but have not publicly renounced and must therefore attend her wedding as to not stir the pot. Besides, your parents have promised dinner at Flo's Clam Shack the day after the wedding. Such culinary displays of fried grease on wax paper at establishments with picnic tables and plastic lobsters affixed to wall netting are now, at your wizened, un-ironic age, your spoils. As is your mother's offer of spending her $100 gift card on you at Target.

It is a bribe. In exchange for new looped, rubber-bottomed bathroom rugs and a mold-free shower curtain, you will have to explain to your mother that you are the last of your college friends to be unmarried, although you won't disclose that sleeping with your boss, who's married, qualifies you as not single, sort of, and that you call your boss late at night, after a few glasses of wine, trying to make his wife suspicious. It was your mother who taught you that¾taking the bull by the horns.

But you were always so popular at school. Your mother will stare at the packaged sheets, taupe-colored, made in Thailand, in the home furnishing aisle of Target, and her memory will be flooded with photos of the cheerleading squad and your modern dance lessons and James Hilliard, who tried to fuck you up the ass in that motel bathroom as you leaned over to pull out your tampon, his curled, half-limp-with-drink penis pushing against the side of your anus wall and making you scream, and maybe it wasn't rape because he compromised and entered you in the correct orifice after you wrestled yourself away from him, upset that your prom press, hanging over the shower curtain, now lay in the tub with the ice and the beer and there was a stain, small, purple, the size of a grape, near the waist that you have not noticed.

He came on the side of your leg and you balled up your pantyhose to clean it. Your mother remembers the corsage James brought you, a corsage with baby's breath, not the one-fifth of skanky tequila he pulled out from the bench seat of the limo and passed around to Keith and Wendy and Nate and Allison before getting to you, chug, chug.

You always had impossibly high standards, she concludes, as if there could be no other explanation. After all, when James graduated from Cornell, he married Allison. You know, the Allison who gave him a hand job that same night, while you were passed out on the motel sofa, your head wedged between the seat cushions, Nate or Keith fondling your breast. Perhaps your standards are, relative to then, higher.

You wonder if you will tell her about Dickey. Dickey, who, like Tommy, disappeared from your life in the sixth grade, when the inevitable college and ordinary guy tracks began to diverge, when the high school guidance counselors penciled them in for industrial arts and budget math and you for algebra and AP biology. Maybe she will be happy because they learned practical things, like fixing a transmission or laying shingles, unlike you, who majored in comparative

Russian literature. Like Boris and Natasha? You imagine Dickey would laugh, rubbing the clean, chemical-smelling grease on the backside of his mechanic's jumpsuit. You clearly see the dirt embedded under the recessed curves of his fingernails. You imagine those fingers touching your skin, scrubbed by Body Shop cucumber exfoliate, and feel the oil leeching your pores like blood through a cloth.

Did Denise know what a period was? What did she think that was every month? Did it scare her, like the baseball scared her when she batted, so much so that as soon as the ball left the pitcher's hand she turned her back toward the mound, pushing her helmeted head into the bat and cowering? And then, when a pitcher from the Dundalk Tigers, accidentally put one between her shoulder blades, she never came to the plate again, even though the coach still let put her in as the left second left fielder. Sometimes Tommy would try to pitch to her, underhand, before the games, but she would stand with one foot out of the batter's box and always dropped the bat and ran when the ball reached the plate. You always wondered whether you, as the only other girl on the team, should have intervened in some way, helped her. But how?

And what would you say to Dickey now? He's in the grocery mart of the Exxon, buying cigarettes. You linger in front of his black Monte Carlo with the orange racing stripes. There's a line of rust eating at the bottom of the fender. You made sure to rent an Audi at the airport. Your parents, like Dickey, have a Chevy. They have always bought American. They live in a neighborhood lined with Cavaliers and Tauruses and F-150s. You hate the blue-collar American-ness of your upbringing, the way they embrace it, with their support our troops magnets and flag stickers and country music stations.

You live in the grayscale of your mind, a watercolor of overcast streets in central Europe, in smoke-stained tube stations and discotechque advertising slicks. You find it hard to believe that you ever had a crush on Dickey, that you ever listened to B-104 and knew every song in the weekly countdown hosted by Casey Kasem on Sundays. You do not know when you started to feel different, when you stopped reading *Sweet Valley High* novels and started reading Sartre, and why your sister never read at all and who votes Republican and attends Toby Keith concerts. You do not know why Denise became developmentally delayed and you did not. You do not know why you fell out of love with Dickey or why you can't seem to leave the married guy and, if you broke up his marriage, you are sure you would not stay with him, not when he's single and suddenly he's shitting in your toilet and leaving his wet towels on the floor.

It is definitely Dickey. His skin is ruddier, his cheekbones inverted triangles that stab at his jaw. The only thing soft, vulnerable about him remains his blue eyes, the color of bird eggs cracked open too soon. He rips the foil off the top of his menthol Marlboro cigarettes and tosses it into the garbage can by the pump, raising his eyebrows at you.

My brother Jerry and I were on the 1982 Orioles, you explain, leaning against the hood of his car. You are wearing a yellow sundress you bought for the rehearsal dinner later tonight.

I remember Jerry. Dickey puts a cigarette in the corner of his mouth. He looks you up and down, and you know what he is thinking: You were such a tomboy. You wore your hair short and got your fair share of "lez" from the opposing players. But you discovered facial hair remover and *Mirabelle* magazine in college, right after you gave up the Dead and the existentialists and became...what?

Nice. Dickey nods, smiling. His grin is lopsided; half of his face looks like the Joker. What was your name again, sweetheart?

You try to smile, nonchalant, but you realize only you have been thinking about Dickey and Tommy and Denise all this time; no one has ever thought of you. You played in your brother's shadow in Little League; your prom date fucked and married someone else. Come to think of it, you were never a maid of honor, barely a bridesmaid. You are even not the protagonist of your own life, of this story. This story you cannot even seem to start.

Alex¾right. You played in left field or something. He leans on one leg, shoving his hands in his pockets of his too-tight Levis.

It is stunning that he would peg you for an outfielder. Doesn't he remember cussing you out at second base when you forgot to tag the baserunner, when Arnold tried to cheer you up after the game and you called him a stupid kike, like the way the other boys did, including Jerry, even though you didn't know what it meant until you read that Salinger story, years later?

Tell Jerry I said hey. Dickey moves slightly to your left, his hand reaching for the door latch of his car. You do not budge, explain you are home for a wedding, that you live in Chicago now, and you've got a few hours to kill before the rehearsal dinner. Would he like to get a drink?

***

It is not a place where you would order a martini, and most of their scotches are blended. Domestic beer and country on the juke box, an inflated Budweiser blimp listing over the square island of bar in a wood-paneled room off the highway. You laugh because it reminds you of the bar in the *The Accused* starring Jodie Foster, but how it is funny that the four or five white guys wearing baseball caps and drinking Coors eyeing you from different sides of the bar might conspire to gang rape you?

She was a fuckin' bitch. Dickey speaks of his estranged wife in between smoke puffs, as if she is dead. They have a child together. You are not surprised its name is Kaitlin. You wouldn't date Dickey in a million years, but you wouldn't date Joe, either, the groom who you will see in two hours, his lumpen boy face and soft beer gut further buffered by his cushy job in financial services. You get married?

You could tell him you have a career. You do, teaching English and composition at a private girl's school. I'm in education.

You ask him if he likes Tom Waits. He looks at you like you are Frankenstein. You dig your finger along a familiar tunnel, a hole so much now it is liable to collapse upon itself. It is all you have shared, really, the 1982 Eastwood Orioles, although you shared countless hours with Dickey in your mind when you were a child, concocting beach dates where you would listen to ELO on the transistor radio and share French fries on the boardwalk, where you played house and made Dickey meatloaf and spaghetti and meatballs because your mother could not make much else, could not introduce you to the world of sushi and bim bop, Vietnamese summer rolls and camembert.

I'm a machinist. Dickey sucks six ounces of beer out of his Budweiser in one take. It's a fancy word for cutting out motorcycle parts. I mean, a machinist can cut anything steel or metal or whatever, but I cut out motorcycle parts.

Did you think you were going to be that, when we were young? The beer has started to make the lights around you soft, turning the garish naked light bulb clipped above the cash register the color of yellow construction paper.

I thought I would pitch for the Baltimore Orioles. He stares at the top of his beer bottle. But I don't what happened. High school, wrong crowd. I never made it past JV. Still, you know my father was a machinist, so I guess if I had to pick something back them, it would be something like that. Except I don't drink away half the paycheck—only a quarter. What's Jerry doing, that sonofabitch? He called a great game—best catcher ever caught me.

Jerry sells boats. Of course, there is a story behind the story, how Jerry majored in marketing in college and got laid off from four sales jobs in five years before getting a part-time job at a friend's boat dealership. Jerry never wanted to be a catcher, never even tried out for JV in middle school; by then, Jerry had grown four inches taller and two hundred pounds heftier and spend most of his time eating pizza in his room and playing *The Legend of Zelda* and the only thing that kept Dickey Richards and guys like him from beating the shit out of Jerry in the boy's bathroom was the fact he called a mean fastball in, cutter away, changeup.

Yeah, no kiddin'—like Bayliners and stuff?

I guess. You have never been in a boat, and Jerry has never invited you on his, a 10-year-old pleasure boat bought with his salesman's discount. The reason you and Jerry don't talk anymore is because once, more than fifteen years' ago, you walked in on him in the garage masturbating. Sometimes you dream you are dating Jerry, having sex, and you wake up and you're grossed out. When you changed the diapers of the disabled men in that summer during college, their flaccid penises the size wider than long, like tuna cans, you thought of Jerry, had to close your eyes and hope you didn't get their pubic hair caught in the adult diaper tape. So do you keep up with Tommy and Denise?

Tommy's dead. Dickey lights his millionth cigarette before offering you one. Didn't you know?

You have been back home three times in ten years. You haven't seen Tommy since your senior year of high school, when you passed each other in the hallway during classes. He said hey¾he was always nice to you, always remembered you¾and you asked him how Denise was. She had gone to a different high school, for special students. Back then, your future seemed as wide open as theirs seemed closed. But you didn't count on setting so many traps, so many roadblocks and mazes for yourself.

He got shot, Dickey explains, and you immediately think drugs. In the line of duty¾foiled a robbery. It was just him and Denise, you know. He took care of her like his own child.

You clench the cold glass of watery beer with both hands. Where would Denise be now? You know the facility where Dickey tells you she was moved after Tommy's death. It is behind the shopping center with the Roses and Rite Aid in it. You did not even know their parents had died, even though they were much older than your own, more like grandparents (and endlessly speculated on by Jerry as the reason Denise was born developmentally disabled). The only time you went to Tommy and Denise's house was for Tommy's 11th birthday party, and it smelled like old people even then. The cake seemed generic, cheap, with a clown on top instead of one of the cooler Superman or Batman cakes, and Tommy let

Denise blow out the candles. He let Denise open his birthday gifts, too, and keep the ones she liked, including the GI Joe figures that he had coveted for months. It seems hardly fair, and you wonder why you have been spared such tragedy, at least for now. Jerry is getting fatter and your sister Amy gets Botox and you are an adulterer. Your parents take vacations in a RV and read Oprah-crowned bestsellers. They have no known diseases.

Tommy always liked you, Dickey says, rubbing your shoulder. You hear his breath, heavy and full of beer, and you wonder how such a cute tow-haired little boy could fill you with such revulsion now. He had a crush on you, I think.

It seems selfish to nurse self-pity from a dead man's crush, to pluck the possibilities—like petals from a flower now blowing lazily along an afternoon breeze—of this revelation. What have you lost that he has not lost more of, that Denise has not lost even more? Should you have gotten Hodgkins in your twenties? Should you have joined the Peace Corps?

It seems important to see Denise now, offer your condolences, even as Dickey invites you back to his place to smoke some weed, and possibly, you think, have sex. If he had not told you about Tommy, you may have, and missed the rehearsal dinner, but his choice of details has changed the trajectory of the entire night, and you marvel how weird that seems, that not even events, but thoughts, things take up no weight or physical space, can alter the course of one's life.

You are glad you got the rental company insurance on the Audi. It won't save your license from being suspended, but since you are a little drunk, it will pay for the damage if you happen to pull out the transmission after running over a curb.

Like Dickey, you know Denise will not remember you. It is only important that you remember her, never forget her. Salvage your own life by changing the trajectory of hers somehow.

* * *

This is how Dickey comes along. When he drops you off in the parking lot of the gas station where you left the rental Audi, it's gone. Your bags, your toiletries and laptop, you imagine, have been dumped somewhere on the side of the road as the perpetrator floors your racing green rental Audi with no low jack up to the west side of town, or maybe he's decided your carefully wrapped sachet of gold and diamond jewelry is the perfect gift for his baby momma in the suburbs.

Probably towed. Dickey points to the posted warning not to leave vehicles for more than two hours. I guess you need a ride to the lot, huh?

Do you mind? You will not make the rehearsal dinner, and worst of all, you will have no good excuse.

Do you mind if we stop at my place first? He presses his nostrils together between his fingers. I need a little pickup.

Dickey lives in a rancher a few miles from the soon-to-close steel mill. Weeds ring the house like upside-down beard, and the sidewalk to the door is more crumbled than a day-old graham cracker. You half turn your ankle and wind up removing your mock-espadrille wedges only halfway to the porch before wishing you hadn't because the carpet feels slightly moist and mostly bare, like airport.

Can't have anything nice, with kids, Dickey shrugs as he flicks on the lights and walks across the living room to the kitchen. His backside is firm and shapely and you wish he would come back naked and maybe if you have a healthy sexual relationship with someone beside your boss you will stop dreaming about Jerry because there must be some

Freudian connection there but it will not be Dickey because in the unflattering fluorescent overhead light of the kitchen you can see his hawkish face, the collapsed areas underneath his cheeks where meth may have paid a visit, the strange reddish color of the outer cartilage of his ears, his slowly eroding hairline. He returns, stepping over a Barbie car and a My Little Pony, delicately balancing a mirror and a baggy of white powder in the crook of his palm. The other hand holds two cans of Bud.

I got my little girl two evenings a week—I don't even bother cleaning up her shit 'cause she just pulls it all out, anyway.

You think of saying how social services might be interested in where he hides the cocaine so that Kaitlin does not find it accidently or that teaching Kaitlin to clean up her own fucking toys is a perfectly valid, welcomed social skill but instead you say oh and he laughs and pats the cushion of the brown suede overstuffed couch.

You want kids? he asks, cutting up the lines to the size of joints and after a snort you are telling him about your theory that you can never have kids because you feel emotionally stunted, that children cannot have children. You can never think of your own mother and father as ever being children. They seemed born into parenthood, and you wondered what happened between generations, why the parenthood gene did not express in you, in others. Sure, Jerry has kids and so does your sister Amy but they both seem the same as they were when they were kids, Jerry with his newer video games, X-Box and Wii and Amy with her stupid crushes on country stars and you with a closet full of *Sweet Valley High* novels that you pull out sometimes and read on Friday nights, trying to figure out what went wrong.

Yeah, babies are having babies. Jerry nods this as some kind of profundity. Pretty soon we'll die off in diapers. To be honest, I wasn't ready to be a father, but Kaitlin, you know, she's mine, my kid? It's so awesome and so...weird. I stare at her like she's from outer space. And then I think, Jesus, in a few years that girl's gonna be smoking hot. Not that I'm a pedophile, but I feel like I was just in eighth grade or something. And now I'm losing my hair.

You want to go visit Denise with me? You appeal to him regarding the nature of her innocence, your combined lost innocence, some Proustian journey that will culminate in a visit to an adult facility and free you from your psychoanalytic bondage and you will be able to start over. Plus, the coke has kicked in and Jesus, it's fucking good.

Dickey insists on bringing Denise a gift, a baseball he has found in the high grass in his front yard, a ball that has a home there as the result of an errant throw from a neighborhood child but now has destiny and agency, a brown-stained, slightly damp and unraveled ball that you wouldn't touch wearing a glove. It rolls around on the dashboard of Dickey's Monte Carlo as he takes the curves of the thirty-mile-an-hour shopping area liberally, his back fish-tailing into the intersections.

Van Halen—you could not touch them back in our day. Dickey lights a cigarette with one hand and turns up the radio volume with the other as you reach over to steer. They were fuckin' Gods up until they made *1984*. Then fucking Sammy Hagar, what was that?

Why did Tommy join the force? You have reattached your espadrilles to your feet, the soles making squeaking noises against the waxy paper of hamburger wrappers, hot rod magazines, and a Disney princess coloring book, which you pick up to study Kaitlin's artistry. To your surprise, she has stayed within the lines and used the correct color palette, no green-face princesses or princes with purple shoes.

He always dug that military shit—remember all those GI Joes he had? He didn't want to enlist though, because of Denise, so he signed up for the police academy. What good that did either of them. I mean, I deserve to be dead more than Tommy. *She's runnin', I'm flyin,' right behind in the rearview mirror now...*

Dickey is a surprisingly on-key singer. He smiles a bunch of teeth at you, in decently good care, and when you roll up to the Middle River Community Living Apartments, you can almost imagine fucking him. No brunch, no follow-up, no exchange of phone numbers and Facebook pages, but something quick in the dark. But maybe it's the coke. Your heart feels like a rabbit's and you almost tear the door off the car trying to get out as fast as humanly possible. Dickie half-squats on the sidewalk, laughing hysterically, his eyes shining into yours in conspiracy, and you put your fingers to your lips as some woman with a fat corgi mix idles by and glares at the both of you like you are hoodlums but hoodlums is the wrong word, as if you are characters in *West Side Story*, and you think maybe trash is the word she glares and Dickey takes your hand and you half run to the door.

The entranceway, where you find Denise's name on the mailbox of 403, smells like piss. It is only then that you think this is a bad idea, but it's only in very small print in the back of your mind and you can barely make out the letters. Why wouldn't your visit be viewed as anything less than you planned it—a charitable, curse-lifting, guilt-absolving, cocaine-abetted sidetrack when you are supposed to be toasting Suzie what's-her-name's good fortune at the Gilded

Room of the downtown Marriott? You open your purse as you ascend the carpeted stairs, Dickey humming Van Halen, and see the green bars of text and phone messages crowding out the screen of your iPhone, your mother and the maid of honor and God knows who else.

It's us, Denise! Dickey shouts after three sets of knocks have gone unanswered. It's the 1982 Eastwood Orioles! It's Dickey and Alex!

Denise, we have a present for you, you add and nod at Dickey, who mock slaps his forehead and nods toward the car, where he's left the baseball. You want to go out for ice cream?

I bet I could jimmy this. Dickey takes out his gas card. This deadbolt's a piece of crap.

You imagine taking Denise out for that ice cream—you noticed a Friendly's as you half-spun through one of the intersections here. You could pretend you are yourself and that Dickey is Tommy that you have always lived together like this, that instead of hurrying away after your perfunctory conversations with Tommy in the hallways, you engaged him in meaningful discussions. Maybe he would have taken you to see the movie *Pretty in Pink*, lied that he enjoyed it, and secretly went home to masturbate to Molly Ringwald. If it was Tommy's penis you had seen first, instead of your brother's, maybe you wouldn't be so fucked up. You would explain, when Denise opened the doors, that you and Dickey are the defective ones, that her smile, simple, broken, the way her buck teeth cut into her bottom lip, would shine on both of you like an epiphany.

Fuck. Dickey sucks on the well between his thumb and forefinger, which he has nicked with his knife trying to slip it under the doorknob casing. You push him away and press your ear against the door to listen. You strain and hear the muffled sound of the television in another room, perhaps the emphysemic wheeze of the refrigerator. You close your eyes and try to send a telepathic message to Denise, that you mean her no harm. You think of Tommy patiently tossing underhanded batting practice to her, letting her open his birthday presents, blowing out his candles. If you could be one-tenth as good as Tommy, you bargain, after this evening, then you would be happy. You could move forward, do the right thing, if you just had some sort of sign.

Get off, you shrug off Dickey's hand as he tries to pull you away from the door. But when he doesn't let go, and you open your eyes, you see it's not Dickey. It's a police officer. It's seems karmic destiny, and you beam at Dickey, who is not understanding the karmic significance at all.

They know Tommy! You practically shout at him. They've come to let us in!

We got a call from this address about an attempted break-in, says the second officer, hand on his belt, unfastening some handcuffs. You need to come with us.

* * *

You do see Denise, as the cruiser pulls away with you and Tommy in it, knees touching, coming down from the coke faster than a kid down a waterslide. You turn in the seat and look through the rear windshield, and she is framed, backlit, like a postage stamp in the window, an elfish woman with chopped gray hair and blue eyes so large she could star in a Rankin/Bass stop-motion production. You have probably done enough tonight, attempting to break into her apartment to take her out for ice cream, to give her nightmares for weeks, to turn back the strides in therapy she has made since her caretaker and protector was killed in foiling a robbery attempt, and you do not understand this reverse flourish of Midas touch you have unleashed.

At the station, with your one phone call, you have to explain to your hysterical mother and have her repeat back to you that she and your father need to pick up your towed rental Audi before she comes to the station and here, you will explain everything, after they fingerprint you and take your statement, decide how to charge you. But how far must you go back to explain everything, to ten o'clock this morning, when on the flight here you had a vodka, even though you are not an alcoholic and certainly only have one drink before work on most occasions, when you vowed you'd rather do anything than go to this stupid wedding, or to the first time your boss cheated on his wife with you or to fat, greasy Jerry during high school, his hand covered with your mother's Jergin's lotion, rubbing his erect penis or those failed promises of those *Sweet Valley High* books, or should you have taken dance like Amy instead of playing co-ed baseball, which both your mother and your father tried to talk you out of, when she arrives, looking sadly so much older than you remembered her, two years ago, at Christmas. It dawns on you that she will die and this will be one of her memories of you.

You have sipped half a cup of tepid drip coffee trying to sober up and gather your thoughts, and your mother says, do you mind, Alexandra, telling me what the hell this is all about, you say she was our second left-fielder. You have to start somewhere.

GREAT WHITE

The last time he'd gone to Nantucket was 1987, and he'd spent that week drunk or fucking Michael Haynesworth. They'd drank so much gin that Charles joked if he ever got cirrhosis of the liver, he'd know which weekend was to blame. Now he sits on the bench inside the Hyannis ferry repositioning his foot in his loafers so that the corn that's grown on the side of his toe doesn't rub against the leather. His six-year-old daughter, Rachel, is creeping her index finger up and down his own, pretending it's an inchworm.

"It's Larry Inchworm," she giggles when Charles looks at her. The last six years of his life have been bookmarked by this look, that of a man who opens his eyes from a long dream and wonders where he is, what has happened to him. When he drank gin with Michael on the deck of the sailboat CALAMITY, when they fucked below deck, he wonders whether he'd thought of the future then with the same alarming frequency he now thinks of the past.

"Larry Inchworm," he repeats tonelessly. When he is in the mood, he will play with her, and play with her good, but right now he's wondering when Rachel's mother Linney is coming back from the concessions bar, where she has gone to buy Rachel an orange juice and him a coffee, whether she is going to throw herself overboard into the choppy waters of Nantucket Sound instead. "When did Larry Inchworm come along?"

Rachel has a lot of friends—Samuel Sloth, Betty Band-Aid, Larry Inchworm. He's not sure whether it's time yet to panic because most of her friends aren't real or whether a healthy imagination is good for a young girl who's already been through so much. He honestly doesn't know; he's never read Dr. Spock—or anyone else, for that matter. His own childhood he has repressed for the most part. He only came into a cup at the office of the fertility clinic, and, at the time, naively, thought that was all that his parental duties would comprise.

"He came with us from Baltimore," Rachel explains, and he takes her index finger, Larry, into his hand. "He's never seen an island before."

It had been Charles's idea to come, as if cordoning them off from civilization would somehow corral Linney's emotional unraveling. Linney, who'd always been so quietly fearless, so resolute, so magnetic in a way of which she was completely oblivious, who he was in love with but not exactly in a way he could explain to anyone else, certainly not the men he occasionally slept with still, even his ex, Jude, who'd known Linney as long as Charles had.

"They didn't have Splenda." Linney is back now, holding the coffee cup, the plastic bottle of orange juice, her dark curly hair slipping out of the knot in which she'd loosely tied it. "I put some Equal in it."

"Did you get anything for yourself?" he asks, relieved she has completed this simple task without a hitch, although he knows his question is rhetorical.

"I'll get something when we get there," she says, screwing the top off the orange juice and holding it out to Rachel. And when they get there, he thinks, she will defer until dinner, saying, perhaps, the ferry made her slightly seasick, and then she will pick at something at a restaurant later that night, just enough to make him happy.

"Did you know Larry Inchworm has come along for the week with us?" Charles opens the palm on his hand and Rachel grabs the orange juice bottle, looking downcast at the table.

"She's doesn't care about Larry Inchworm," Rachel complains, and Linney, as if to inadvertently prove Rachel's point, is staring into space, revisiting, he's sure, her own past, wondering what Marti would be doing if she were here, if she were alive, what she would be wearing, whether she would be giving Rachel the orange juice or discussing Larry Inchworm. Marti, who Charles knew he could not bar from the island but hoped would not come out of Linney's suitcase, her makeup bag, her heart, while they were there.

"Who's Larry the Inchworm?" Linney smiles at Rachel, a mixture of surprise and interest, but Rachel has already brought the orange juice to her mouth and guzzles as if starved with thirst, tipping the bottle so high so that some escapes its mouth and drizzles onto her chin, her neck, and Charles must grab a napkin from Linney's outstretched, floating hand and stem the small deluge before it reaches Rachel's new pink-striped sundress.

***

"It's beautiful." Linney stands in front of the clapboard house, a mile inland from The Jetties, her elbows out, hands pressed against the small of her back. The cedar shingles covering the house have faded to gray, as have all the others on the island. Charles thinks the town looks washed out, Stepford-like, reflective of all the old stodgy conservatives, like his parents, who spend the summers here; the housing board thinks they are part of its charm. "It's hard to believe you haven't come here for years."

"My mother was still alive," he jokes. And after she'd died, after she was no longer around to make him feel like dogshit on her shoe, he broke up with Jude and was never in a relationship long enough again to want to bring anyone up.

When she doesn't answer, Charles walks past her, fumbling with the keys, his garment bag, Rachel's rolling suitcase with the Disney princesses from *Frozen* on it, forcing the key into the lock and jiggling it to the left, turning right. The smell of lilac and lavender and other beautiful things that his mother had kept in the house fill him with such longing that he stands in the hallway, wondering if he will hear the click of her sensible Pilgrim pumps on the slate floor of the kitchen and the rich, full sound of them on the hardwood as she crossed the kitchen into the hallway to meet him, before she told him, instead of giving him a hug, that his pants were too tight or his collar open too wide, or that his father was already at the golf course, even though Charles had never played golf, never would, would prefer to take tea with his mother and gossip about the other gossips who'd driven up for the summer from the Upper West Side or Connecticut or flown from Texas and, even though she hated it, preferred he be drinking Tom Collins on a boat in the Sound with some Upper West side blond, or even, for Christ's sake, some artist from Sarah Lawrence. He was her only child, after all, and she secretly liked to gossip with him.

"It's gorgeous." Linney steps lightly down the hallway, her fingers trailing along the wall. "I'm sure Marti would have loved it."

"I'm sure," he repeats, going back onto the porch to get the rest of their things. Linney grew up in southern New Mexico at a hippie hostel. It was Marti who introduced her to things, like 19th-century furniture, who gave her a job at the opera company and then gave her her heart. He was fond—very fond of—Marti. He even loved her, albeit more like a sister and not in the slippery way he loved Linney. And it was tragic, her cancer. But if he had to hear her name once more this hour, today, he was going to put Linney on the ferry back to Hyannis and gossip with Rachel for the next week over slow gin fizzes about Larry the Inchworm.

"Mommy, when are we going to the beach?" Rachel has come into the house. She had lagged behind, poking around in the dirt in the garden, and before Linney can answer, Charles sweeps Rachel up in his arms and whisks her away to the powder room off the main hallway to wash her hands.

"We can go to the beach in an hour," Charles says as he scrubs Rachel's hands with an ancient, hard bar of soap, as yellow and shiny as scrimshaw. "Why don't you show Larry Inchworm the back yard?"

"Can I pick flowers for Mommy?" Rachel holds her hands high and far from her body as Charles dries them off.

"Of course." He wonders what is out there. He knows his father pays the landscapers, someone to clean the house once at the beginning of the summer season and once at the end. Did they keep the deep blue mophead hydrangea that she loved, the pink hollyhocks, the white roses and lavender?

When they step out of the bathroom, he is pleasantly surprised to see that Linney has taken some of the bags upstairs. When he and Rachel follow, he is even more surprised to see that Linney has picked Charles's old bedroom, full of nautical maps and model ships, for Rachel to sleep in instead of the guest room. He envisions sitting at the edge of his old bed at night with her, going over the countries on the maps, and where the ship models that line several shelves across from it would sail, based on their construction and size. He thinks she might particularly be interested in the whaling ships, but wonders if perhaps she won't, because he will have to explain that the whales were hunted and killed. He worries about his instincts as a father. He wasn't as involved in her early years, when Marti was there, when there were ballerina tutus and Barbie dolls and tea parties (although he could handle the latter).

"This was Uncle Charles's room." Linney turns to them as they enter. She is holding one of Rachel's t-shirts, still folded in a square. "He slept here when he was a boy."

"You were a boy, Uncle Charles?" She looks up at him with astonishment and perhaps respect.

"When I didn't want to be a little girl," he wants to say. There are so many things he must catch himself saying before he says them. About being gay. That he is not her uncle, but her father. He and Linney have broached the subject only briefly among themselves about the best time to tell her, whether it had been the right decision even to withhold it from her at all. After all, if she had been expected to accept having two mothers, why couldn't she be expected to welcome a father into the mix?

"Yes, he was the cutest little boy." Linney bends and clasps Rachel's shoulders. "And now you and Samuel Sloth and Lenny Inchworm can sleep here just like he did."

"*Larry* Inchworm, Mommy." Rachel shrugs her shoulders, herself, away from Linney.

"You want to pick flowers with Rachel?" Charles suggests when Linney looks up at him helplessly. Linney wasn't always like this, he thinks. Not even in the first year after Marti died. She went to work, took Rachel to preschool, and played with her at night in her room. She soldiered on, a numbness that had set in months before Marti even took her last breath in their bedroom. But the numbness had begun to thaw, and it seemed the longer Marti was gone, the harder it was for Linney to convince herself that she was somehow coming back.

Complicated grief, a psychologist friend who taught at the same university as Charles had explained. But Linney was already seeing a therapist. And she had dived back into her work as director of the opera company, Marti's old job, before coming home a tired shell, a woman who walked about the townhouse, through its rooms, as if she lost something or had forgotten why she had entered them. Maybe Charles, trying to be helpful, had indulged her in her grief by taking care of most of Rachel's day-to-day needs. And when he tried to give them back to Linney, he was horrified when she would fail at them, forgetting to pack Rachel a snack for kindergarten or not scheduling off work to take her in for her pediatrician visits or simply not listening to the endless chatter of Rachel's life, not knowing Rachel's favorite enchanted fairy from that show she watched or that she wasn't friends with her friend from preschool, Moira, anymore, although Charles wasn't sure exactly why that was, either.

But she hadn't argued when Charles had suggested they go to Nantucket this summer instead of Rehoboth Beach, where she had always gone with Marti and Rachel. He is still holding onto this little victory, and he will drag it all the way to shore this week like a great white whale.

Downstairs he pulls from the grocery bags the Stoli and Beefeater and wine he'd gotten at the Stop and Shop at the inlet before they'd driven out to the house. He feels around in the ice maker and claws a large glacier of ice out of the bin, dropping it into the ice bucket. He needs this vacation, he thinks, just as much as they do. His last book, about a doomed relationship between two male fur trappers, was rejected by thirty publishers before he told his agent to stop shopping it; he's been single, mostly, since breaking up with Jude over a decade ago. He has a bum knee and can no longer play tennis twice a week at his club. He's become a parent; his days of being a top in the bottom of a sailboat are well behind him.

But he has plans; he's hoping to get up to Provincetown one day this trip, to wear his lapels wide, his shorts tight, and maybe he will get laid or at least get a look. Even the latter would be a boon for his confidence. If he can just trust Linney alone with her own six-year-old.

He makes himself a gin and mint, watching Rachel and Linney through the window. If he is lucky, Rachel will forget about the beach for today, and he can slowly slip into a comfortable place, carry the buzz through the evening, be in his own warm, faraway place. Just like his mother. He frowns at this memory, setting the glass on the counter, and glances around the kitchen before deciding on a compromise. He adds another splash of gin to his glass and takes the glass outside in the yard, joining Rachel and Linney at the hydrangea bush.

"We should wait until morning to cut these," he advises, taking the shears from Linney. He's surprised he remembers so much about their care. "And only the most mature flowers. Let's try some asters instead."

***

"Which bedroom do you want?" Charles asks. They are standing in the hallway. Rachel's been asleep for an hour, almost two. At the Miacomet Golf Club Restaurant she had tried her first lobster roll, and Linney had picked at her salmon while Charles had a couple more gins and a sirloin.

"It doesn't matter," Linney shrugs. "I put my bag in the guest room."

"If you want..." he nods toward his door, and she nods back, heading down the hall. He showers and lays atop the sheets of his parent's queen poster bed, leafing through a copy of *Harpers* he'd bought at the airport until Linney comes in her nightshirt and climbs on the bed next to him.

They sleep together sometimes, in the same bed, since Marti died, but they've never slept together. However, they have crushed on each other at different points in their lives, Linney first, when she was a freshman at Hopkins and she'd taken his Intro. to Romantics class. She hadn't realized he was gay and actually thought he was asking her out when what he really was asking whether she'd be interested in walking his and Jude's dog. Linney, in need of money more than a boyfriend, took the job. And when she moved in with them after she'd flunked out of school, for a time, before he kicked her out, it was like a whacky, Mary Tyler-Moore era comedy show.

He had crushed on her later, when she had visited him again in his office at Krieger Hall. She was no longer the coked-out mess she'd been when they'd parted less-than-amicably seven years before. She wore a skirt and a fashionably cut blouse, her wild curls neatly tucked into a bun. She'd gone back and gotten her bachelor's in graphic design at the

Institute. She was working at the Baltimore Opera Company and dating the director, a woman Charles's age named Marti. A woman with whom she'd wanted to have a baby. Because of Marti's health history, Linney had agreed to carry their child. But she wanted the father to be someone she knew, and Charles thought, as he sat at his desk twirling his grading pen, that more than anything, he wanted to draw Linney into his arms, gaze into her light jeweled eyes, and kiss her.

"You wouldn't have to be involved at all if you didn't want," she had assured him, her delicate, pale hands clasped in her lap. "After you donated. Although I'd very much like for you to be."

But they had never slept together. Still, they laid between the sheets and talked about their days, and the first few months after Marti's death she clung to him like a buoy, crying herself to sleep, crying herself awake, shell-shocked she was not yet thirty and already a widow with a child.

"Rachel wants to be a sea captain now," Linney laughs as she turns to face him in the bed.

"As well she should be," he answers. "Shall we begin reading her *Moby Dick*?"

"I don't know about that," she says. "But maybe we can get her some books from that little bookstore I saw in town."

He is not attracted to most women. And he knows that if they did sleep together it would probably break them apart. The attraction, he thinks, for him, at least, is that they are off limits to each other. And yet they are the closest to each other of anyone. Even before Marti died, much to her chagrin, he was Linney's second opinion, her sounding board, her bitch session. Linney is like his mother, in a way. The only difference is she actually loves him.

She cradles his face with her hand and smiles, dreamy. Her softness is real, but there is a hard seed within her that you could break your tooth on if you bit too hard.

"We're going to have a great time," she says, and he nods. He can't believe her; she's said things like this so many times before. But he stretches his lips into a smile, makes sure she sees it, before he turns off the lamp on the night table.

***

It's never sweltering on the island, which is why it's such a draw. Still, the walk to the Jetties is exhausting; he wonders how he ever wandered up here as a child, when, after breakfast, his mother showered and her first martini prepared, shooed him off to the beach alone with a blanket and a tote bag full of plastic toys.

Linney walks ahead, Rachel lags behind her, and Charles picks up the rear on the uneven dirt and gravel road. Every so often a car rolls by and they move to the edge near the cattails and rocks. Rachel had collected quite a few of them in her plastic bucket until the handle began to buckle and she set it down every few feet. Charles wills Linney to turn around and notice the bucket, command Rachel to either jettison her load or offer to carry it for her, but she doesn't. She has slipped into that ethereal space, where ghost Marti is walking alongside her and they are talking about the fall production of *The Pearl Fisherman* or *Carmen*, or about what they will make for dinner.

Charles wonders if this is okay for Rachel. After all, he'd survived, alone, every summer from when he was six, his mother not caring about child molesters or sharks (and by the time *Jaws* came out in 1977 he spent more time on the beach in his Speedo, showing off the two curls of hair on his chest, the bulge between his legs, than splashing in the water). Rachel would learn to adapt. Linney's mother had left her and her father when Linney was four and she had adapted, just as he had. But maybe it was because of that Charles wanted Rachel to have what they hadn't.

"Mommy, I'm tired," Rachel pouts, stopping. Linney turns, pulling her straw hat low over her face so that it rests atop her sunglasses.

"Sweetie, we're almost there." Linney smiles and waits for Rachel to catch up to her. "My God, where did you get so many rocks? Where are you going to put all your seashells?"

She takes the bucket from Rachel with one hand and adjusts the folding chairs she has draped over her shoulder, taking Rachel's hand with the other.

"I bet there are mermaids in the Sound," Linney says to her. "Do you think we'll see any?"

"No," Rachel answers. "Uncle Charles said there were whales."

"But they're thirty or forty miles offshore," he interjects. "So we probably won't see them from the beach."

"How about seals?" Linney glances at him.

"They're on Muskeget Island—it's between Nantucket and the Vineyard. They have tours and such for both."

"We should definitely do them," Linney says. "Won't that be fun, Rachel?"

"Yes, but I want to see mermaids at the beach," she answers, and Charles is relieved and annoyed. Relieved that they won't have to spend a day out at sea on a touristy excursion and annoyed that Linney has put the silly mermaid idea into Rachel's head.

"Did you have to go on about the mermaids?" he asks when they are settled, under a rented beach umbrella, Rachel twenty feet in front of them plunging her bucket into the tepid surf.

"Oh, it's just make-believe." Linney pulls her book out of her tote bag. "It's no different than the enchanted fairies. Would you rather buy her more Band-Aids or mermaid dolls?"

Charles laughs aloud. Every week for months, it seemed, Linney had to buy a box of regular-sized Band-Aids from the grocery store so that Rachel could make her Band-Aid family—little faces on one end, with a tie or a lacey neckline in the middle to signify Bert or Betty Band-Aid, and their slew of children and pets. And sometimes Rachel would put the Band-Aid family on herself, on her fingers or elbows or ankles, and take them to preschool, where they would get lost or ruined during play or given to other children that Rachel alternatively longed for and loathed.

"Touché." He glances at her book. It's one of Marti's books, Jorge Luis Borges' *Fictions*, an English translation. He fishes out the thermos in which he has made himself mojitos and takes a sip. "I didn't know you were a fan of Borges."

Linney pretends not to have heard him. He knows that it's too early for Linney to start dating again, but he knows her pretty well that she never will. Marti was her first love, probably her only. She gave Linney normalcy, security, after she'd lived so many years in her early twenties alone, desperately poor, in a roach-infested efficiency, a college dropout, and estranged from her father, clinging to sobriety. But it's a security, Charles thinks, that Linney has mistakenly attributed to Marti, and that her self-possession has been with her all along. It was probably what Marti, thirteen years older, had been attracted to. It was what attracted him, certainly.

If Linney's white whale was Marti, than Charles's surely was Jude. And he was determined to find someone, even just a flirtation, in Provincetown. His life was not over. And maybe if Linney could get herself together, back to being a mother, he could get his own life back on track, maybe even move out. Start another novel instead of helping Rachel write little stories about her Band-Aid family on his laptop.

He had been the one who insisted on being Uncle Charles.

"I want to be in your life again," he had said that night in his office. "Assuming your life is back on track—which it appears to be. But I don't want to be a father. I never have. I can be her uncle—that way, I can still be in her life."

"I'll take it." She stood up as if, he thought, to shake his hand. But she came around his desk and pressed the length of her body against his, her head on his shoulder, and her sigh was so deep he felt it press against his own chest. "I've missed you so much."

That had worked fine until Marti's cancer came back. Suddenly, he was living with them, helping Linney with Rachel as Linney took care of Marti, through her surgeries, her chemo, her radiation, her home hospice, taking over her job as director of the opera company. And although he had never wavered when she asked, had never thought of himself then, he wondered why he didn't. Especially when he was thinking about himself so much now.

"I think I'd like to go to Provincetown for the day," he floats it casually, after he's taken another sip of mojito.

"Are there things there for children?" Linney asks, not looking up from Marti's book. "You know how she gets."

"Well, I was thinking that—I'd go alone."

"Oh." Linney puts the book down and looks at him in embarrassment. "Of course. I'm sorry. Of course you'd want to go alone. I'm sorry."

"Don't be sorry." He touches her arm. She has such a way of making him feel like a heel, even when she doesn't mean to. "I just wanted to get back in touch, so to speak."

"Would you spend the night?" She presses. "I mean, of course you can. I just wanted to know whether I needed to plan."

"I don't know." He hadn't thought about what would happen if someone gave him a look. "I mean, I'd call you."

"Of course." She digs into her tote bag for her water. Linney stopped drinking after she got into Narcotics Anonymous. "You know, you don't need my permission. If you ever want to go out, you can just do it."

"It's not that." He glances at Rachel. She has set two wet, amorphous mounds of sand together with her bucket.

"We'll be fine." She notices him looking. "I feel relaxed already."

"Well, that's great." A wave fans inward, quickly, to the shore, and Rachel jumps up in surprise, her mounds now small bumps. "That's good to hear."

"I had a dream last night about Marti," she continues. "I mean I always do, but it was about the trip. She had driven to Rehoboth, but we had driven here. And I drove all the way back, so upset that we had left her, that we'd miscommunicated."

"Did you bring her to Nantucket?" He scratches his knee, trying to keep his expression blank.

"I don't know—it was right before Rachel woke us up." She holds the water bottle a few inches away from her face, lost in thought.

"Was she mad?"

"I don't know." She shakes her head. "And that's what is so awful. I'll never know anymore."

"I'm sure," he starts, but there is what he wants to say and what she wants to hear. "I'm sure she with us the whole time. You just never realized."

"Shit." She thrusts the water bottle into his hand, standing up. "Where's Rachel?"

Before he can answer she is already gone, toward the water. Charles wants to stand, run after her, but his legs feel like they're in quicksand. He'd only taken his eyes off her for a second. He doesn't breathe again until Linney reappears in his vision, her fingers laced around Rachel's arm, above the elbow. Only then he is glad, hopes it is a lesson.

***

He decides on the A-House. It's one of the oldest bars, the most traditional, and, as a writer, he always liked to stare at the nude photo of Tennessee Williams walking along the beach that hangs in the bar. There are actually three bars in the location, one of them leather, but he was never much into that. He grabs a stool at the Little Bar, where most of the locals hang out, and gets a gin and tonic. He's wearing a crisp new button-up he'd bought at Vineyard Vines earlier that day when he took the ferry over to Martha's Vineyard with Linney and Rachel. He splurged on himself but also on Rachel, buying her two stuffed mermaid dolls with shiny green tails, one with brown and one with blond hair, like her mommies. He also bought several books about ships and a little board game called Mermaid Island. They sat in the living room with Rachel and Linney when Charles had left them early in the afternoon, taking the car on the ferry back to Hyannis and then driving up the Cape. Of course he would have to stay the night because it was so far, and he'd be drinking. He'd have to get more than a look.

He sips his drink and glances at his cell phone. Of course, Linney would not call him but he thought of calling her, telling her how fun it would have been if she could have come. He misses Linney the fag hag, for sure. Even though she didn't drink, she would happily hang out the rare nights he wanted to cruise, pointing out the men she thought he would approach. She would pretend to be his sister and once his wife who was just, as she'd told a surprised personal trainer back in Baltimore, "cool with her husband's lifestyle." He was surprised that Linney had settled into domesticity so quickly. But he had lived with Jude for ten years. Did he want to live with another man for ten years more, or did he just want to go back in time and live with Jude, who had been living with someone else for seven?

"It's a little chirpy in here." The man who has slid onto the stool next to Charles is older, maybe early fifties. His hair is greyed at the temples, closely shorn, wearing a polo and madras shorts, sandals. He's referring to a group of men by the fireplace who have broken out into a Cher song. "What are you drinking?"

"Gin." Charles shifts sideways on his stool, spreads his legs a little and grips the sides with his legs. "Charles."

"Derek." The man winks. His face is marble, etched by laugh lines and wrinkles. "You in town with your boys?"

"I'm just here for the evening." He puts his cellphone in his back pocket.

"That's a quick dock." The man smiles and waves some bills at the bartender. Derek is an accountant from Connecticut. He comes for a week in the summer. He's a year out of an LTR. Not that it's important that Charles know all these things. He knows they will never see each other again after tonight. But what little time he has, he drinks it all in—the ropey muscles of Derek's tan neck, the smell of his aftershave, Drakkar Noir, his Nautica polo. A little too preppy, and not much of a reader. Jude was a playwright, and Charles's Edward Albee jokes were more appreciated, at least understood, with him. But it's not about that right now. It's about his dick stirring in his pants and all the pent-up frustration that may geyser out of it before the night is through.

"This is better than talking about Larry Inchworm," he says after a few drinks, somewhat to himself, but allowed.

"I'm sorry honey, did your last sweetie have a teeny?" Derek laughs, his thigh pressing against Charles's.

"No." Charles shakes his head. "I have a six-year-old daughter down in Nantucket." And this is where it always gets complicated.

"I thought you said you lived in Baltimore," Derek is confused, but not alarmed.

"I do—I'm on vacation with my daughter and her mother. We're not married." He waves his hand. "But we live together. It's complicated, but it's not."

"It's only complicated if you make it." Derek's breath tickles Charles's ear, and for once, he agrees.

***

He is lying naked in a hotel room down the street, studying the goosebumps on his legs as Derek lies with his back to him. He was out of practice, for sure, last night, but like riding a bicycle, some things you never forget. He feels the looseness of his limbs, the fact that they have slept in, unlike at home, where Rachel wakes them up at ungodly hours each day to eat breakfast and watch cartoons. He thinks about Saturday mornings in bed with Jude, having a bloody Mary to take the edge of the hangover that set its small hammers against his temples. How he might write in the afternoon, or maybe they'd go to the farmer's market or a matinee show at the Charles. Life had arranged itself around him like a heavy comforter, and he was happy never to have to venture out into the cold, dim room. He'd thought about growing old with Jude, traveling the well-worn grooves of their lives, the album old, popping and crackling, not mind-blowing like the first listen, but still a song that made them nod their heads, snap their fingers.

He'd hated Jude for cheating on him, for pulling away those bedcovers and showing him the paunch of his stomach, the knobbiness of his knees. For making him wonder whether anyone else would find him desirable, whether anyone would ever want him again.

He sits up and picks up his cell phone off the night table; there's a message from Linney. His heart feels like a water balloon. He opens it and is relieved to see it's just a picture of Rachel and her dolls. She is out on the deck, hugging them and also one of Charles's toy ships. RACHEL WANTED ME TO SEND THIS, SORRY. Linney has typed. It was sent last night, around nine o'clock. He wonders if Rachel is worried that he never responded, where he is. He pulls on his boxers and pads over to the door of the hotel room, leaving it open a crack as he steps outside.

"She's fine," Linney says cheerily. There is a sound in the background, a blender. "Enjoy yourself."

"Are you fine?" He presses the phone closer to his ear. One night he'd come home from class to find Rachel in the living room, crying, clinging to Chester the Pug. He'd found Linney unresponsive on the bedroom floor, an open photo album, a spilled water glass, and his bottle of Ambien.

"Of course—why wouldn't I be?" A dish clangs, maybe a fork. "Who's the lucky guy? Are you going to spend the day in Provincetown?"

"His name is Derek," he answers, and laughs. He'd never thought of himself as a Derek person. "If you need me to come home—"

"We're going to take the bus into town and go to the whaling museum," she cuts him off. "Anything else you'd recommend?"

"You could stroll along the pier," he answers. "But you know how she gets when she's fussy. Be sure to bring the cheese crackers, not the peanut butter ones."

"I know, Charles," she says this line softer. "I know. Just let me know if you want us to meet you up at the ferry. I think that last one's a six, right?"

"Are you mad at me?" He glances back into the room, wondering whether he can get his things and go.

"Only that you haven't told me all about Derek," she laughs.

"Maybe there'll be more to tell later," he concedes. When he steps back into the room, Derek is sitting up, the blanket draped casually over his waist.

"Coming back to bed?" He grins, pulling back the thin white sheet. It's cold in the room, dark. A feral, sharp scent weaves through the air.

"I'm starving," Charles answers. "Brunch?"

* * *

The older Charles got, the harder dating had become for him. Although he's sure it's hard for anyone. Still, things that seemed so easy when he was younger—attraction, sex, conversation—became less like shooting the arrows of his desire into an open field of bucks and more like aiming for a bullseye the size of a nickel.

But he is not dating Derek, he reminds himself as they stop in a furniture shop on Commercial Street after brunch.

"I'm not a huge fan of modern," Charles says as Derek sits on an ottoman that looks like it's constructed from the rubber of bicycle tires. But would he be, if a man were promising enough? "My daughter's mother—she has a nice collection of Chippendales. Of course, they were her partner's, but she really grew into them."

"I just like what I like." Derek shrugs, his hands in the pockets of his khaki shorts. Last night he tried to give Charles a hickey.

"It's good philosophy to have," he concedes. "When my mother died and my father downsized, he went to Ethan Allen. My mother would be turning over in her grave, but to him it was just furniture. There was always more."

"So what's your deal with your daughter's mother again?" Derek asks as he handles a nautical-themed lamp.

"We're co-parenting," he answers. "We live together. At least for now. I mean, her partner just died, and she's not in a good place."

"Sounds like you have a lot of your plate." Derek glances up at him.

"It wasn't a problem last night," Charles points out.

"For you, or for me?" Derek places the nautical lamp back.

***

It's four o'clock, and Charles is in that comfortable place. When he was with Jude, it happened a little later in the evening, after dinner and a few martinis at Central Station, but it's that place in which his brain feels like taffy, and so does time. He doesn't have to worry about being a less-than-midlist author, about whether Jude will take that job in Seattle and force him to give up his tenure. All that matters is this drink, and maybe the next. There is no vast, tumultuous sea; there's only merriment at the inn, a hearty dinner, a bed in which to pass out.

"When are you heading back to Nantucket?" Derek asks when the bartender places his palms on the bar in front of them, their empty drinks. "Don't you need to catch the ferry?"

"I should, but I don't know whether I can," Charles answers. Or whether he wants to. Whether he wants to go back to Baltimore at all. He wonders whether he can wait tables at the A-House for the rest of the summer. His knees aren't that bad. He can live frugally, drink rail liquor.

"Well, I was thinking of going down to the Shipwreck." Derek places his credit card on the table. Whether it's an invitation or departure, Charles isn't sure.

He thinks of Linney that night on the floor, when she'd said she'd taken a handful of his Ambien.

"You signed up for this," he said as he ran a cold shower for her, after he'd gotten off the phone with poison control. "You're a mother. You don't take the day off because you're sad."

But it hadn't been all bad. It just was the ebb and flow in their vast sea together. Still, it was hard to tell whether they'd gotten too far or too close to anything.

"I don't know what to do." He looks into his glass, tipping it to his lips. He sucks the last bite of gin and lime out of the ice cubes.

"Well." Derek stands up. "You know where to find me when you do."

He knew Jude had been cheating on him for years—three, at least. But he'd never confronted him. They still led their lives, and Charles had hoped, after one fling had ended, that it would be the last. It was Jude who left, finally, with a dancer named Stephan. He took their Volvo, although Charles kept the apartment, one he was still paying the rent on, even after he'd moved into Linney and Marti's almost two years ago. He didn't know why he still kept it—he didn't imagine anyone moving in after Jude, but he couldn't ever envision himself moving out, either.

***

At the ferry terminal in Nantucket, he can't find Linney and Rachel. The pier is awash with tourists, in Vineyard Vines polos and sundresses and sandals, and it is hard to see through the throng, but he has the sinking feeling that something has happened. Of course it would, he thinks, because he left Linney alone. She is incapable of basic responsibilities. Rachel needs him, he thinks, more than ever. He pulls out his cell phone and hits Linney on his speed dial, his eyes slits beneath the cup of his palm, scouring the wave of bobbing heads that streams around him on the pier. The phone rings once, twice, three times. His patience presses tight on his chest, his jaw.

As he walks down Broad Street he sees them, coming out of the ice cream shop, Linney with a cone in either hand. She holds up her hand to signal him and nudges Rachel, whose face is melded to her own cone, toward Charles.

"Hey." Linney smiles, holding out one of the cones to him. "I got you rum raisin."

He takes it from her, watching the ice cream begin to drip down the cone. He needs to act fast, but he is paralyzed, by the busy street, the still-bright sun, Linney's smile, the faint scent of Derek's cologne near Charles's collar.

"I got cookie dough," Rachel announces, jarring him out of his daydream. She has eaten hers down to the cone already. "We saw whales today."

"At the museum," Linney clarifies, as she digs into her bag with her free hand. She pulls out a ticket envelope. "I got tickets for the whale watch tomorrow for Rachel and me."

"The whale watch?" Charles laughs in disbelief. How is it, he thinks, that he's even angrier? "Do you know how long those are? You can't even—"

Linney blinks; her lips part. They both look at Rachel, who looks at them, curious. Charles wonders if she will remember this when she grows up. How angry he was when he realized they didn't need him after all.

"You can't even invite me?" He smiles, squeezing Linney's shoulder.

"I didn't think—" Linney stutters. "I didn't think you wanted to go."

"I do." Charles is not sure he does, either. It's a six-hour trip. He pictures them, motoring through the Massachusetts Bay, out into the Atlantic, without him.

"Well." She looks down the street when he doesn't answer. "I think they're still open. I might be able to get another ticket. Eat your ice cream—it's dripping all over you."

Charles squats beside Rachel as Linney makes her way back to the ticket office, even though his knees hurt, his hands sticky. He smells the sweetness of the ice cream on her face and hands, her sweat. She has his nose, or, he thinks, she will.

"So what did Larry Inchworm do today?" He smiles.

"Larry drowned in the ocean yesterday," she answers disinterestedly, biting into her cone. "Inchworms can't swim."

***

The whale excursion tour guarantees sightings, although Charles knows there's no such thing as guarantees. Even on a six-hour tour.

"The Minnow was only a three-hour tour," Charles jokes to Linney as they climb onto the double-hulled boat. He grips Rachel's hand as she begins to pull him to the front platform. "You know, Gilligan's Island? The shipwreck?"

"I never saw it," Linney answers. She's lugging the tote bag packed with their lunches, suntan lotion, Rachel's mermaid dolls, light coats. "I guess ignorance is bliss."

"It was a terrible show," he says, as he positions himself behind Rachel, who's leaning over the front of the rail. He wonders if she will move from this spot in the next six hours, whether his knees will hold. He decides not to think that far ahead. "I envy you."

Charles grips the railing as the boat chugs toward Stellwagen Bank National Marine Sanctuary, Rachel bobbing in front of him, up and down on her tippy toes. Linney grips the rail as well with one hand, adjusting her sunglasses, her hair pinned under her sunhat. He wonders if the whales will scare Rachel if they see them, whether they will get sprayed. He wonders if he will be awed or disappointed, or just sunburned. As they clear the dock, the land, the water spreads out, smooth, aquamarine, before them, darker and choppier with foamy caps closer to the boat. The air, sprinkled with salt, slices through his hair, underneath his sunglasses, making him squint. But he can't look away. He is in the best spot, in the best position, to see.

EAT A PEACH

Lynn always waits near the far end of the farmer's market in West Hollywood, in the food court. That way, she can see the women before the women see her. If Lynn gets a bad vibe, or just a case of bad nerves, she can slip out to the parking lot and drive away. Her sister Lucy thinks it's strange that Lynn treats these outings more like drug deals than the blind dates they actually are, but given Lynn's bad luck, it's the only way she can get herself (halfway) out there.

"She doesn't sound like a catch," Lucy said on the phone last night of Rachel, the woman who Lynn is meeting today. Lucy is married and lives in the Atlanta suburbs with her husband and children in a five-bedroom house, the kind you see on cable shows, clean but soulless, with quartz countertops and en suite master bathrooms.

Lucy is usually right about most things, and as Rachel enters the food court and navigates the maze of tables, both hands gripping the strap of her purse, eyes squinting, body closed, like a tourist in a Tunisian marketplace, Lynn presses her sandaled feet on the ground, ready to bail into the throng of Saturday shoppers. Rachel's online profile was full of red flags—widower, young daughter, not necessarily ready to feeling like she should wade back in a little. But again, Lynn's own life on paper—massage therapist, axed credit cards, barely affordable studio apartment in Echo Park—is nothing to crow about, either.

Lynn watches as Rachel scans the faces of those in her immediate area, her lips slightly parted, and something about her expression, the soft glassiness of her green eyes, the haphazard way her hair curls over her ears and a little in her face, makes Lynn stay a minute longer. She knows this is a mistake—but this private moment of Rachel's vulnerability tugs at her. She lets Rachel find her, watches her face lock into a smile, one hand unattaching itself from her purse to give Lynn a quick, enthusiastic wave.

"I was just coming to meet you," Lynn lies, standing up. She leans over and hugs Rachel with just her fingertips. "You look exactly like your picture."

"You too." Rachel holds onto Lynn's forearms. She keeps her close for a second. "Your hair's even redder in person."

"It's the sun," Lynn says. The picture she used for her profile was taken indoors, her face shadowy, lit by candle. Her friend Michael said it made her look mysterious and artsy.

Then, she doesn't know what to say. It's been a long time since she's let it get this far. There was Yuki, who she slipped out on, fearing she was too trendy and possibly shallow, and Kim, who had too many tattoos. And Sandra, who she simply stopped talking to on the dating site because she'd discovered a sixth degree of separation between Sandra and her ex.

"Something came up, by the way," Lynn lies. Even when she lets it get this far, she always builds herself an out. "A last-minute appointment—so I only have about forty minutes. I hope that's okay."

"Well, we'll just have to make do," Rachel says a little too brightly, and Lynn can't tell whether she's disappointed, whether she knows Lynn is lying. "So, do you have time to grab lunch, or just walk around?"

Rachel wears real perfume and not essential oils. Her makeup is so bare Lynn can see a light smattering of freckles, the faint lines of crow's feet around her eyes. She's definitely in her late thirties, as listed on her profile, five years older than Lynn. Her TOMS look like she's walked a thousand miles in them, and Lynn gives her bonus points for thinking ratty canvas slip-ons were fine to wear on a first date.

"We can do both, I think," Lynn reassures her. Maybe she should have given herself an hour. She has aborted so many trips to the Farmer's Market she's never actually shopped here. That, and Ralphs is more her price point. She puts on her straw hat and sunglasses and walks beside Rachel toward the Littlejohn English Toffee stand. The girl behind the counter offers them hard, flat, sample squares of toffee. As Lynn bites into hers, she watches Rachel wrap her sample in a napkin and slip it in her purse.

"For my daughter, Maggie," she explains. "I always feel guilty, going out without her."

"How old is she again?" Lynn asks. She hears Lucy, slightly nasal, on the phone. *You've never wanted children, Lynn. You're going to take care of someone else's?*

"She's seven," Rachel answers. Her skin is pale, like Lynn's. She hides it under a faded denim button-up, her neck swaddled in a scarf. "She was five when Deborah passed away, and she still worries when I—I'm sorry, I shouldn't be talking about this."

"Why?" Lynn's throat is still thick with sugary toffee. "It's your life."

"So, you're a massage therapist?" Rachel glances at a text on her phone before dropping it into her purse. She smiles at Lynn. "You're a healer."

"I wouldn't say that," Lynn laughs. "More like a body mechanic."

She did a semester at community college in North Carolina, then massage therapy school in Studio City. She was surprised that she liked massage, touching stranger's bodies, kneading their pressure points, freeing them from pain, their own self-imposed stresses. She was worried she'd have to offer words of comfort, of understanding, but most people don't want her to talk at all, only listen. Most of the problems—cheating spouses, budget overruns at the studio, the actor who is a liability—she wouldn't know how to solve, anyway. Her friend Michael, who she moved here with, says the only problems people have in LA are the ones they make for themselves.

"You're the healer," Lynn says after a moment. "Working in oncology."

"I always thought I'd be a concert pianist," Rachel answers. "But life took some detours. I would have never met my partner if I'd been a concert pianist."

"Was she an oncologist, too?" Lucy is almost screaming into Lynn's ear now. *Run, don't walk, away.*

Rachel looks straight ahead. "She was my friend."

"I'm sorry." Lynn touches Rachel's wrist lightly. She doesn't have to date Rachel, she thinks, but she can be sympathetic. She understands loss. She understands things being ripped away from you.

"I knew she was terminal." Rachel says the word 'terminal' like 'left-handed.' "And I thought at the time there was no way I would get involved. I mean, what did I think...but I wouldn't have had Maggie if I hadn't."

Rachel stops in front of a produce stand.

"Want a peach?" She holds one in each hand. "First of the season."

Lynn holds the velvety fruits in her palms as Rachel pays the vendor. She wonders if they start dating whether they will celebrate every year together by going to West Hollywood and buying peaches at the farmer's market. Her last girlfriend, Alex, a midlist actress with a recurring role on network show, was a big fan of traditions. They always went to the same place in Sherman Oaks for brunch, and when Alex wanted to break up with someone, her new girlfriend began showing up everywhere—as if she had always been there, the old girlfriend an illusion. Six months ago, when Lynn showed up at Alex's apartment in Woodland Hills for a party, Sherrie was already there, in the kitchen, opening a bottle of Chardonnay, Alex's arm encircling her waist.

"To spring." Rachel holds up her peach and takes a bite. She smiles as she chews, her eyes slightly squinted again, along with her nose. Lynn bites into hers. It's not completely ripe, the meat tough near the pit. But it's not Rachel's fault, she thinks, the state of California produce.

"My ex is an actress," Lynn says. "I came here to LA with my friend to get away from North Carolina because it was pretty conservative, but I've had a hard time meeting people."

"It's hard to meet people anywhere when you're older," Rachel agrees. "I spend most of my time with people who are dealing with life-altering situations, and I'm guessing you spend your time with people who are hurting in so many ways, too."

Lynn wonders what it would be like if she were the one speaking for once. What she would say. What it would be life if someone rubbed her shoulders, knuckled the back of her neck to relieve her headache. To release the heaviness from her heart. She wants to burrow in some corner of Los Angeles and start a garden, have a small yard and a cat. She doesn't want much. In a city where there are so many fantasies, she wants a reality. Her sister Lucy would tell her to move back home, and Michael would tell her to dream bigger. She wants the in-between.

"How's your peach?" Rachel is nearing the pit of hers. Lynn glances down at her own, at the small ridged oval made by her teeth.

"It's good." She opens her mouth wide and braces as the bland meat fills her mouth. They stop at a stall selling hot chicory coffee and beignets. Lynn wonders if the vendor thinks they're friends or if they're dating. Rachel stands close to Lynn; she touches her forearm lightly to point out interesting items on the menu board. Now that Lynn is single, she always wonders when she is at a restaurant or the movies whether the other people around her are on first dates, trying to pretend they are like everyone else. It's the same thing she started thinking after Lenny—whether, as she stood in line at Starbucks or Target, whether those around her were grieving. What they held down, like a beach ball in the ocean, to keep from rising to the surface.

At the table in the food court Rachel stirs her coffee and glances at her phone again.

"My daughter," she explains before putting it away. "It's the last time, I promise."

"If you need to get home…" Lynn starts. She doesn't want to ghost Rachel. But she will let her ghost herself. It is easier to lose momentum, she thinks, then to gain it.

"No, no." Rachel reaches across the table but stops short of Lynn's hand, her words quiet but firm. "I'm not going anywhere."

Lynn studies Rachel, her crooked smile and disheveled curls, the smudge of beignet powder on the corner of her lower lip. She feels some chemistry between them. At least comfortableness. She wonders if she could lie about her made-up appointment, say that she canceled. But then maybe Rachel would figure out she lied in the first place. Another red flag, if they are keeping score. Besides, Alex used to tell Lynn that people built narratives out of the thinnest of threads. A drafty door in a house where someone was rumored to have died made one think it was haunted, or, meeting the eyes of someone across the restaurant who was simply looking for the bathroom, love at first sight. The mind built the narrative one wanted, regardless of the facts. It was why, Alex explained, she was an actress. If she spent her time on the set building narratives, she could be completely honest on her days off.

I don't love you, Alex told Lynn the first night they'd slept together. *I will never marry you, and I don't believe in soul mates. But if you want to hang out and sleep together, I'm totally into that.* Still, Lynn had hoped for something different—and where had it gotten her?

"I need to go soon—I'm sorry." Lynn dusts the powder from her own beignet off her fingers. It takes a moment, the beignet was so rich—and she wishes it could take longer. She wants to inventory the moment, to test how she feels: Deborah. Maggie. Grief. Uncertainty.

"Already?" Rachel looks up. She leans back in her seat, her lips taut. Finally, she smiles, almost apologetically. "Well, I had a really nice time—I hope you did, too."

"Of course." Lynn also nods, standing up. She hugs Rachel lightly again and grabs her peach off the table, pretending she will finish it. Instead, she will throw it away in her apartment, discreetly, uneaten, wrapped in its napkin so that she doesn't begin to smell it in the trash can a few days from now. She stuffs it in the drink holder in her Yaris and is halfway home on East Beverly Boulevard when her cell phone rings. She glances at the caller ID: *Rachel MD*. Her hand hovers over the vibrating phone. Did she forget her purse? She locates it, with a glance, on the floor of the passenger side. Still, she answers.

"I'm sorry," Rachel says. Lynn can hear traffic through the phone speaker. "I just got into an accident, and I didn't know who to call. I'm so sorry."

"Oh my God." Lynn grips the steering wheel with her other hand. "Are you okay?"

"I think so." Her voice trembles. "But my car—I just called for a tow. I'm sorry. I don't even know where you are."

"I'm right here." Lynn flips on her left turn signal. "Where are you?"

She finds Rachel standing on the corner of Beverly heading west, her Passat station wagon angled across the intersection, the right front door crushed into the passenger seat and pushing against the tire. Lynn pulls into a metered spot and, before getting out, stuffs the napkined peach into her purse. Rachel's left hand cradles her right arm as she speaks into the phone to someone. When she notices Lynn approaching, her face softens, and by the time Lynn reaches her, she is crying.

"I'm so sorry." She mouths to Lynn, and then also to her: "Insurance."

Lynn nods. She rests her palm against Rachel's left forearm and studies the Passat. It's light blue, the color of sky. She wonders, if they start dating, whether they will tell people the story of their first date at the farmer's market, each of them careening away in opposite directions on Beverly when fate T-boned them back together. The other vehicle, a dark gray muscle car, is owned by a young Hispanic man with a pencil-thin moustache. He strokes the crumbled, gleaming hood like it is a baby that he's trying to lull to sleep.

"Oh, Lynn." Rachel drops her right hand by her side, turning toward her. "I'm so sorry. I didn't know who to call. I mean, I guess could have called one of my friends, but I wasn't thinking—you must think I'm crazy."

"No," Lynn says. She is too confused to think anything. "Just unlucky, maybe."

Rachel sniffs, nodding. Without thinking, Lynn brings her hand to Rachel's face, wipes away a tear with her thumb.

"It's pretty lucky that you were right here." Rachel smiles through her tears.

***

Lynn's ex, Alex, always liked to play games. When they had coffee at the café down the street from Alex's place, she'd look up and grin mischievously.

"Let's improv," she'd say. "Where are we headed?"

"In this relationship?" Lynn would muse. At the time, their relationship still early, Lynn was still optimistic.

"Or after this coffee, even." Alex would clarify. "We head to LAX and...where do we go?"

"Tokyo," Lynn offered. She'd always wanted to go to Kyoto.

"Or Brazil," Alex interrupted, her eyes flashing, so dark they were almost onyx. "And sunbathe on Campeche Island. So who walks up the beach toward us?"

***

Lynn wonders now, after the tow truck comes and she drives Rachel back to her home in Beverly Grove, what will happen next. "Blue Sky" by The Allman Brothers comes on KLOS.

"This song is from *Eat a Peach*," Lynn says to Rachel as she waits to turn left onto South Robertson. "If you believe in coincidences."

"I didn't used to," Rachel answers. "But after the past few years, I feel like I really don't know anything."

"My older brother had this album when I was little," Lynn continues. "I always thought it was an orange on the cover—but of course it was a peach, I mean, it's in the album title. Anyway, I'd always ask Lenny, my brother, to play the orange album. And he'd make fun of me."

Lynn doesn't know why she tells the story—to make Rachel feel better? But then she remembers bringing up coincidences.

"I don't know if I believe in coincidences, either," Lynn says. "Maybe your mind connects dots to make sense of things."

"It's right here." Rachel touches Lynn's forearm and points to a Spanish-style house. "You can just pull into the driveway."

Rachel gets out of the car without saying anything. She waves to a little girl with dark hair at the front door and then glances back at Lynn. Lynn gets out of her Yaris and reaches Rachel just as the little girl, presumably Maggie, does.

"This is Mommy's friend, Lynn." Rachel explains after Maggie hugs her. "Mommy got into an accident on the way home, but I'm okay."

Another woman, in her late teens with thick dark hair, appears in the doorway.

"That's Lenore," Rachel murmurs, her lips are close to Lynn's ear. "She babysits sometimes."

Rachel pushes Maggie gently toward the door, and it's understood that Lynn will come too. If Rachel had asked her to come in, Lynn figures, she would have been able to decline. But now Rachel is holding the door for her, and Lenore recedes into the shadows of the house and there is nothing to do but get swept in.

"Mommy, are you okay?" In the hallway Maggie clings to Rachel's leg like a buoy in the water. Her hair falls in dark ringlets onto her shoulders. "Are you going to die?"

"I'm fine, sweetie," Rachel laughs. "Patty got a big boo-boo, but she's okay, too."

"Where's Patty?" Maggie asks as Rachel opens her purse and pulls out her wallet.

"Patty is at the dealership," Rachel answers, and Lynn is relieved. It's now obvious she's talking about the car, Patty Passat, not another child. Or another woman. Lynn is surprised she cares so much about the latter.

Rachel pulls out a twenty and a five and holds them out to Lenore, who slips them into her jeans pocket.

"I'm so sorry," Lenore says. Her lips at rest curl downward at the edges, like a permanent sulk. "Do you need anything else from me?"

"No." Rachel seems completely removed from all of them, somewhere else, maybe still at the scene of the accident or even an older scene of tragedy. "Thank you." Suddenly, as if remembering she's not alone, she smiles at Lynn. "I'll make some tea."

The kitchen is a galley, but wider than an apartment galley, and all white. Sun streams through the windows as Rachel takes jars of loose tea from the cabinet. Her hand goes suddenly to her neck as she grimaces.

"Here." Lynn places her hand on Rachel's right trapezius and squeezes softly. Rachel exhales through her whole body before she takes a long, relaxed breath. Lynn squeezes harder, finding the trigger point on the top leftmost side of Rachel's shoulder blade. When Lynn hears Maggie come into the kitchen, she stops.

"Maggie, honey, Mommy has something for you in her purse," Rachel says, not turning from the counter. "Why don't you go see what it is?"

Lynn's hand hovers over the denim of Rachel's shirt. It is an amazing coincidence, she thinks, that she's a massage therapist. But anyone, she thinks in the next moment, can rub someone's shoulder. What is real? What happens next? She imagines Lucy scolding her for even meeting Rachel in the first place. *And then it was literally a car wreck,* she can hear Lucy's hard, twangy laugh. Lucy, who was never unsure about anything, who never wavered, even when it came to picking nail polish colors. Lucy always knew what happened next because, like her wedding, honeymoon, and two children, she planned everything in her life down to the last detail.

"My appointment," Lynn says finally. "I should go."

"Oh, no." Rachel turns around. Her face is close to Lynn's. "I totally forgot. I'm so sorry. You're late."

"Don't apologize." Lynn steps back. "It's fine. I'll check on you later, okay?"

Rachel nods, blinking her eyes. On the way the way to the door, Lynn sees the photos scattered throughout the living room—Rachel, Maggie, and the woman—Deborah. In some pictures, Deborah's hair is blond and full, her chin and cheeks rounded. In others she wears a headscarf, her eyes deep in their sockets. On every table, and even the ledge on the white Spanish-style fireplace, there is a photo.

"So I'll talk to you later?" Rachel confirms in the driveway, cradling the back of her neck again. "I feel terrible. Please let me make this up to you."

"It wasn't any trouble," Lynn laughs. She is running away but not to anything in particular. A theme in her life. Driving home, she's reminded of what she hates most about LA—it's hodgepodge of neighborhoods that fold one into the other without any real delineation, every intersection anchored by a gas station and a two-story strip mall with a Thai place/ Korean BBQ/sushi restaurant. She wants clearer choices. She wants to know when she's crossed one threshold and entered another.

When she gets home, she pulls out the water-stained copy of *Eat a Peach* from the milk crate by her stereo and puts the vinyl on the turntable. She found it in the used bin at Amoeba Records on Sunset for three bucks. As "Ain't Wasting Time No More" fills the room, she thinks of her brother, Lenny. Like Lynn, he ran from things and not to them. Except when he died in a car accident, he'd been on his way to look at a motorcycle, a 1979 Triumph, something he'd wanted ever since she could remember. Maybe today's accident had been a warning to her, an omen.

She lies down on her futon couch and closes her eyes. Once Alex had dragged her to the Scientology building to take the Oxford Capacity Analysis test. *For fun*, Alex said. Lynn didn't remember many of the questions on the test, only that they were many, maybe hundreds. One of them was "Do you rarely suspect the actions of others?" which, because she was convinced Alex was cheating on her (she was), she answered no. Unsurprisingly, she scored as being in "an unacceptable state." Alex, of course, had scored as being in "a desirable state."

She doesn't realize she's been asleep until she feels her phone vibrating in the back pocket of her jeans. *Rachel MD*. She stares at the caller ID for a long time. She feels Rachel's shoulder on the tips of her fingers, the soft faded denim of her shirt. She remembers the light floral notes of her perfume, her smile. She then recalls something else about her results on the Oxford Capacity Analysis test: *You scored less than average, and you obviously have great difficulty solving problems.* She drops her phone onto the rug by her futon and closes her eyes again, Gregg Allman singing *Crossroads, seem to come and go, yeah*. Rachel doesn't leave a message.

***

A few days later Lynn's at work, Massage Envy, on Santa Monica, when the flowers come—orange birds of paradise with white orchids. *I feel so awful about Saturday*, the card reads. *Please let me make it up to you—Rachel.*

Lynn owes her the call, she thinks, only because the flowers were expensive. She has already deleted her profile on the dating site, Rachel's number from her phone. Still, she looks up the number of Rachel's office at Cedars-Sinai Cancer Center and leaves a message with the receptionist.

"I had our office manager call all the Massage Envy locations in LA," Rachel explains later that afternoon on the phone, when she calls on her break. Her voice is light, hopeful. "I hope that wasn't too stalker-ish of me. But I wanted to thank you properly—even if you weren't interested in getting together again."

"I'm sorry." Lynn traces an old coffee stain on the break-room table with her finger. What business did two sad, lost people have together? "It's not that I don't like you. It's just...I don't know."

"I understand." Rachel's voice isn't closed, but it isn't open, either.

"No, you don't." Because she doesn't understand, either. Why she has come this far, to the other side of the country, and then no further? Maybe, she thinks, it's because she's run out of room to run. Maybe she has been running to something this entire time. Maybe she is already there.

She's in the drive-thru of the bank that evening when she smells it. The peach, still in her purse. She holds the dried, stained napkin in her hands and carefully unfolds it, like petals on a flower. The skin of the peach is flaccid and wrinkled. She touches her tongue to the orange flesh, and its sour pungency needles her taste buds like an electric shock.

Then, before she loses her nerve, she eats the rest of it, the juice sticky on her lips and fingers. Her eyes water and sting, and she wonders if she will get sick, as the flesh dissolves on contact with her tongue. She holds the pit in her fist, feeling its firmness underneath the slime and stringy pulp. She thinks how strange it is that something could grow from something so hard or, even, how things grow at all. *When you're not looking at them*, her mother used to say to her about the strawberries in their garden. *That's when they grow*.

What happens next? When Lynn arrives at South Robinson twenty minutes later, Rachel's Passat sits in the driveway. A shiny new passenger door reflects the early evening sunset. It was almost as if, Lynn thinks, nothing happened at all. And, depending on who tells the story, maybe nothing will. Lynn puts the Yaris in park in front of Rachel's house and waits in driver's seat. She's not going anywhere. At least not yet.

I'M SUCH A SLUT AND
I DON'T GIVE A FUCK

Hello, Spokane. You peer into the darkness. You could play your first album in your sleep, but you start with the new stuff. You didn't promise anyone anything—even Brian Wilson doesn't sing about t-shirts, cut-offs, and a pair of thongs anymore. Does he?

They haven't come for you. They came for 1994, when you and all those other bands were kinda famous. They came to remember how uncomplicated their lives were, full of promise, because promise is light as air, before it becomes a real thing, rocks in their pockets, in their shoes, so much of what they thought they wanted, doctorates, marriage, children, mortgages, now weighing them down.

Your new songs are in different keys, not bar chords (in your time away, you actually learned how to play the damn guitar). They're about different things, too. About your brother dying and about the drunk kids who come into the diner after the bars close and think it's funny that you were that chick on MTV (they've seen YouTube videos) and somehow it's justification not to tip you or (in their more brilliant moments of sophomoric fuckery) write I'M SUCH A SLUT AND I DON'T GIVE A FUCK on the tip line of the check instead.

Your songs are also about how, after thirty, thirty-five, forty, there is so. much. loss. Your childhood home. Your cats. Your parents. Your coworkers. Your marriage. Your meniscus. Your hearing. All those things that no one wants to hear about—they paid thirty clams to escape those things, to hear I'M SUCH A SLUT AND I DON'T GIVE A FUCK and you haven't even included the song on the set list but you know you'll have to give in before the end of the night and not just because of that guy right in front, wearing a vintage TAMPONS t-shirt who's been yelling it since you stepped onstage but because that's what they're all here for. Even you. You came for 1994, too.

Nobody goes in this thinking they'll do it forever. When you were up here, twenty years ago, yelling into a microphone that you're high or that you're going burn it all down, you did think that, were that, then, but now you have a lump in your breast you can't afford to have checked out and here you are, singing onstage to 200 people, 1800 fewer than in your heyday, because you have other bills to pay, like your student loans (fucking still), your rent, and what were you thinking? You make so much more waiting tables. Was it your ego? Did you have something to prove?

I got old, you say after the smatter of claps for the new song.

Even though it feels like a funeral up here you have to surrender to it, your opus and your curse, and during the second encore you take a breath and strum those chords, strum them like you did in your off-campus house in 1992 that you shared with five other people and two dogs—Jerry Garcia and Smegma—when it was all stoopid and fun, you were so high, just writing songs for each other. You and your girlfriends taped it on your boyfriend's four-track so you could play it again later, for a laugh. You had ne'er a thought about the things that would come to define you.

You are not a slut. You give a fuck. About the three times you miscarried, how you were diagnosed with diabetes. You give a fuck about your brother's brain cancer, and how in the end in hospice he looked like a folded-up lawn chair in the bed. He wore a diaper and didn't know who you were. He died in the thirty-minute interval you'd fallen asleep in the vinyl recliner next to his bed, after you'd bent over him for ten hours, feeding him ice chips, telling him it was okay to let go and his eyes had that mottled, wet, cloudy look that old people have, not forty-year-olds. You give a fuck that you haven't saved for retirement, that you haven't found the one, that you have lost your taste for refined sugar.

* * *

I'M SUCH A SLUT AND I DON'T GIVE A FUCK. You close your eyes, and you remember the oily smell of hashish and the dusty patchouli incense and the dog hair that covered the Guatemalan blankets that covered the burn holes and cum stains on the couch in the off-campus house, and you remember a little of who you were then. It wasn't all that bad. You never see those people now, you never go to reunion, but you felt so alive. Like something you did could actually matter.

You want to be that cautionary tale to that sixteen-year-old girl with her own band, MAXIs, who snuck in, and explain to her that it's not worth it, it's fleeting, it's an illusion of control, like building Los Angeles thirty miles from the San Andreas fault. Nothing is forever, you want to point at her in the back and yell, not my tits, not my ass, not anything.

THE COMPANY OF STRANGERS

Your brother, Clay, is your only living relative in the world, the only one who's watching out for you, who would take a bullet for you, who let you stay here at his place in Truth or Consequences, New Mexico, for the summer, and you thank him by almost sleeping with his girlfriend.

Of course, it's not that simple. To you, anyway. But it seems pretty simple to him when he comes home early from Albuquerque, where he'd gone up to sell some of his custom-made leather holsters, and finds you two in his bed, in various stages of undress.

"Nothing to talk about," he says, packing your clothes in handfuls, soft denims, modest white bras, and limp cotton tees, into a black trash bag. His fingers carry the scent of leather oil, and the thought of never smelling them again is what makes you tear up, not your impending homelessness, your immorality, the fact he may never speak to you again.

You want to tell him that Ginny is the only person who's ever looked at you this way—in any way, actually. You've never considered yourself attractive, and at 20 the fact you've never had a boyfriend—or girlfriend—is more than confirmation bias. Your basketball scholarship from Arizona State pays your tuition but doesn't confer any special status. In fact, there is so little glamour in the Pac-12: shooting drills, overnight bus rides that you spend listening to Martina McBride on iTunes, staring at cacti and mountains and an interchangeable string of Chevron stations. Wrapping your shoulder with K tape, your fingers with surgical tape, packing your ankle in ice. The miasma of leather, rubber, and sweat.

***

You watch your brother underhand both trash bags—one with your clothes, the other with your shoes and toiletries (you had the good sense to grab your laptop and phone charger before he could pack them) from the door onto the broken flagstones in front of the house, about 20 feet from your silver Ford Escort. When Ginny joins him in the doorway, in a half-buttoned Western shirt and jeans, she wears a frown and folded arms.

"Casey doesn't have no place to go," she argues. "I'll go stay with Veronica."

"You're running away to Veronica's after trying to sleep with my sister—that's what you're going to do?" The muscles under your brother's shaved temples ripple and push his Bailey upward almost off his head. He stares into the middle distance, as if trying to comprehend what has just happened—his girlfriend's infidelity, his girlfriend's infidelity with his little sister, his little sister who was his little sister but who now must seem like a stranger in his company after all these years.

"You stay." You hold up your palm to Ginny, as if you have any say in the matter. "I'm going."

There are motels just outside of town, on either end of I-25, but they're small and mildewy and methy and filled with dudes who are ex-cons on their way to becoming cons again. No place for you, your white pancake of a face, your freckled arms and chest that look like your parents sprinkled cinnamon on them.

You pack the trunk of the Escort with your trash bags and head over to Roman's, the pizza place where you have been waiting tables and making pies for delivery when it's slow. The owner is Betty, not Roman, and as far as she can remember, there have never been any Romans as owners or employees. But, as you have found in the weeks you've been working here, histories are like clouds, moving and morphing and oftentimes just disappearing altogether.

"You're early." She stands behind the counter.

"Our wi-fi's out," you lie, opening your laptop on a table in the back, one of six tables (and only two ever filled at the same time). You don't know what you're doing, just trying to look busy, buying yourself time to think, to let your brother cool off. Not that you think he'll cool off by tonight, or tomorrow, or even this summer. And you can't text Ginny, not right now, and what would you say, really?

You think of the time, three years ago, that Clay brought Ginny home to your parent's house in Wyoming for Thanksgiving. You were a senior in high school, shy and unsophisticated (still are), but that didn't stop you from staring at her from the sofa, across the table, in the side mirror of Clay's crew cab while he drove to the store. Even though Ginny was from Texas, her languidity and ease in her own skin, unlike you in yours, made her exotic, intoxicating. Her eyes, so blue and heavy lidded, settled on you with a weight of knowing, her laugh airy but cracked, as if everything you said was interesting and funny. She knew a lot about gemstones and horoscopes and Tarot cards, things that are forbidden by your church, but she brought you some lepidolite she'd gotten from a mine in San Diego and polished smooth. It's calming. She pressed the stone into your palm and closed your fingers over it. It'll help you sleep at night. You looked up at Clay to see if he was rolling his eyes, but his lips were taut, his hand rubbing the back of his neck, and he looked like he'd found a new religion.

One night during their stay, you awoke to Ginny sitting on the edge of your bed in the dark, the pungent and sharp smell of whiskey causing you to hold your breath. She held an unlit cigarette in one hand and stroked your bare calf with the other. Under the sheets you gripped the lepidolite like it was your own heart, heavy and detached. You lay motionless until she sighed, got up, and left. You told yourself she wasn't that way, and you weren't either. That she loved Clay, that she wasn't a cheater.

Your dad was, though—a cheater. When your parents died in a car accident a few months before you graduated high school, Clay and Ginny came back to help out. There had been no money from the sale of your parents' house—your father's feed store carried debts, and there were other unexplained expenses relating to hotel rooms, restaurants, jewelry, and women's clothing. You weren't sure whether you were mad at God for taking your parents or exposing your father's sins or both, but you accepted a basketball scholarship from Arizona State and never looked back, majored in business in the hopes, since you were a sturdy but unspectacular power forward, you could become an accountant, a position in which no one could keep any more secrets from you.

Still, Clay told you his home was always your home. And this spring, before your junior year at Arizona ended, you called him and asked whether you could stay over summer break. Next summer, you would be moving away, more likely than not, for grad school. You were so close to really being on your own, no longer having a coach or faculty advisor or resident assistant, that you wanted to feel like you belonged to something still, even if your family tree now looked like a horizontal two by four. You knew you would see Ginny again, Ginny who you thought of when you cradled the lepidolite at night, reached for it during the day in your pocket. You'd loved Clay so hard throughout your life it made your fist clench, it made you grimace, and you were happy for him but you were curious, curious what Ginny saw when she looked at you, stroked your calf, and you didn't know what would happen, but you certainly invited it, driving out here to Truth or Consequences.

"Two large pepperoni!" Betty calls over to you as she hangs up the wall phone. You tuck your laptop in the safe and pull on a pair of latex gloves, deciding that maybe you can sleep in your car, just for tonight, in the parking lot of Roman's. You need to open the restaurant tomorrow, anyway, so it won't look suspicious if your car is in the lot before Betty's. You'll just have to move it sometime tonight, maybe near the dumpsters but maybe not, since there are some real homeless in town, and they have been known to try to open up the dumpsters, dig out leftover pizza and mozzarella sticks. You wish you'd been thinking more clearly and grabbed one of Clay's Derringers. (As if you'd been thinking clearly at all that day.) You know how use and clean them; in Wyoming, every kid, girl or boy, has held and shot a firearm, no different than learning to drive a car. But you're also glad you didn't give Clay another reason to be pissed at you.

You roll the dough front and back, side to side. You roll it so thin you have to start all over again, and you hurry up so Betty doesn't fire you. The money you make for the month you'll be here isn't much; it'll feed you and with any luck will buy you a new pair of Nikes before training camp starts in August. But you can't live in your car until then. And Betty, while competent enough to own a small business, is, like most small business owners, full of loose screws. She's retired, almost as wide as she is tall, and has a preference for pink sweatpants with words like "Sassy" emblazoned across the bottom. She owns more firearms than Clay and shoots a round from her Remington every night into the sky in her yard before she goes to bed. Her Chihuahua Pappy disappeared a few months ago, and she's convinced that a Mexican gray wolf got her. But you don't understand what discharging live ammunition every night will solve, except possibly hitting you when it comes back down. Still, her other Chihuahua, Loco, hasn't gone missing, but that dog's as crazy as Betty, and everyone gives it a wide berth, probably even the wolves.

"Can you take those out to the hostel?" Betty orders you more than asks as you slide the large wooden spatula under one of the pizzas 20 minutes later to ease it out of the oven. "Hop called in sick; more like he got the drinky-drinky from his disability check, lazy son of a bitch."

You've never done delivery, but the hostel is harmless. It's on the east side of T or C, a bunch of trailers and mineral baths anchored on a stretch of the Rio Grande that attracts hippie-dippy types from everywhere. As if to prove its own point, when you pull onto the small gravel lot by the river, a bearded man wearing a straw hat and a tie dye with a wizard on it waves to you.

"How's it goin'?" He digs in his wallet and hands you a twenty. "These pies are about to hit the right spot."

"I put extra pepperoni on these." You don't know why you did, but you did (probably some universal atonement), and you don't know why you tell him you did. The way the wizard on his shirt stretches over his belly tells you he's probably had a fair share of deli meats in his life. He's maybe in his 40s, but the way he rocks on his bare feet, his white, hairless legs poking out of his cargo shorts, makes him look younger.

"Well, I thank you kindly." As he relieves you of the pie boxes, he leans inward as if to let you in on a secret. "Wanna burn?"

"I gotta get back to work." You shove the money in your pocket. You also get drug tested before the season starts. Not that you've ever smoked marijuana. Heck, your family, except for Clay, who likes his whiskey neat now and then, were purer than the Mormons. But you're not exactly in a place to judge right now.

"That's cool." He rubs his biker's beard. "You gotta make a living."

"I could come back after my shift," you offer. You don't want to be alone with your thoughts. Pizza man, despite his blue, buggy eyes, seems safe enough. You don't have Clay's Derringer, but you have a pocket knife in the glove compartment of your car.

"Well, all right." He nods as if in contemplation. "When you come back, ask for Walter."

***

The hostel is lit up at night like you imagined, with paper lanterns, a couple of tiki torches lining the flagstone walkway that connects all the trailers and leads to the mineral baths that overlook the river. Geckos are painted on the sides of trailers, are set in stones in mosaics. Incense and marijuana alternately greet your nostrils you as you wander along.

"You bring a bathing suit?" Walter is standing in front of trailer 9, wearing a pair of bright-yellow board shorts that rope somewhere underneath his massive belly. He holds out a bottle of Bud Lite and you take it, studying the fire pit in the center of the complex, the girl who's about your age strumming a guitar, a long strand of hair clinging to her bottom lip, partially opened. You are an alien here but, without Clay, without a place to call your own, you're strangely free now to move about, enjoy the company of strangers.

Another man steps out of trailer 9, wearing a Hawaiian shirt. He's taller and heavier than Walter but moves with more deliberation, almost a delicacy. He cocks his head at you in curiosity.

"Casey." You wave with your beer, realizing you haven't introduced yourself to Walter, either. "Casey Hailey."

***

"How unusual—your first and last name are androgynous." He pulls a snack pack of peanuts out of his front pocket and shakes a few into his mouth. "I go by my initials— TJ—Theodore James. Are we heading down to the baths?"

You follow a few paces behind Walter and TJ. You're not sure what to make of them and not sure if TJ is complimenting you or not. But now that you've almost kissed Ginny, kissed a girl, kissed someone, period, you're not even sure what to make of yourself, either.

What did you come here for? Before you can answer yourself, the baths appear before you, overlooking the Rio Grande.

"We come out here every right, right after dinner." Walter sits on the edge of the stone bath, the heat from the water rising in clouds around him, before sliding in. He ropes his arms around the lip of the bath, holding a bottle of Bud Lite and a pipe bowl in the other. "Best view in the southwestern United States."

It is pretty. Out across from the Rio Grande looms Turtle Mountain, which got its nickname from a rock formation on the top that looks like a turtle lying on its stomach. Inner tubes tied to the dock a little way down from the baths bob in the current. You dangle a foot in the mineral water, taking a sip of the beer, watching TJ step out of his rubber sandals and unbutton his shirt. His hair is curly, white-blond, and thinning, a neat mustache anchoring the bottom of his face. His thighs are soft and wobbly as he presses his hands on the edge of the bath and slowly swings his leg, straight, like it's a construction girder, over the tub wall. He's older than Walter, both of them so much older than you. But they've seen something in you, the same way Ginny did, and you'd like to know what it is.

"We travel three times a year," Walter explains. "We've been to 48 states. But I think we're gonna keep coming back to T or C. You've got a nice little town."

"I'm not from here, either." You've rolled your jeans up and let the water lick your smooth, bare calves. It's unbearable, the heat, for a second, but then your muscles spread and relax like batter in pan. "Right now, I'm not from anywhere."

"Well, my friend." Walter lifts his arms, embracing the air, and laughs. "Wherever you go, there you are. Wherever you're from is where you left last."

"Are you trying to say Casey is from the pizza shop?" TJ says this dryly, as if he's engaged in this round of logic with Walter before. He tosses more peanuts into his mouth.

Walter looks at you and wriggles his eyebrows. He holds another beer out to you, even though you're only a third of the way through your first. You wonder if he wants to get you drunk, get you back to trailer 9.

"Did I take my Crestor?" TJ asks Walter.

"Yes, you took it at 4 o'clock," Walter answers. "Two hours before the pizza."

"I don't remember that." TJ sips his Bud Lite.

"You took it when we were in Silver City, remember?"

"Oh, right." TJ looks at you. "Did you know the government designed Silver City without accounting for storm water? They tried to fix it by raising the sidewalks, but a flood swept through anyway and destroyed everything. You know what they say—we're from the government, and we're here to help."

"Mind you," Walter interrupts, "he can't even remember taking his Crestor on those very high sidewalks. Do you know who has to check his pillbox every night?"

You smile. Not only at the story, but because it's obvious that Walter and TJ are a couple, and you are in the clear. You hold out your hand for that second beer, even though you haven't finished the first.

***

You visit Walter and TJ at the hostel for the next two nights, sleeping in the parking lot of the hostel, sharing leftover mozzarella sticks and fries as they highlight their travels to White Sands, Elephant Butte, and, of course, Roswell.

"It was a nuclear test surveillance balloon from Project Mogul." Walter pulls a joint out from behind his ear. "Had nothing to do with aliens."

"That's what the government wants you to believe." TJ cracks open a pistachio and throws the shell out toward the river. It disappears in the stones along the shore before making it to the water.

On the third night, you tell them about Clay walking in on you and Ginny.

"He's the only family you have," TJ says. "You have to try to make amends."

"Sometimes your family isn't blood," Walter says. He looks out over the river, quiet for the rest of the night.

Your brother thought he knew you. And you thought he knew you, too.

"Casey plays basketball at Arizona State," he'd tell Judy, the waitress at the Main Street diner. Or Lorena at the post office, where you helped him mail holsters to customers: "Casey's the first in our family to go to college." Your life was a promise on his lips, as feathery and impermanent as a cloud.

Like clouds, what is known is always changing. New variables are added. New information is discovered. And maybe you don't change per se but become more of who you will be. Either way, you hadn't planned to hurt Clay. You weren't even thinking about him, which of course is hurting him, too, but you were thinking about Ginny. Maybe not even her—you were thinking about yourself. How alone you are. How you wanted to feel something, someone. When she left your room that Thanksgiving at your parents' house, you cried. You knew what Ginny felt but couldn't act on. You've spent your whole life trapped by things you never did, words you never said. You've spent your whole life feeling the ache of longing, confusing it for being alive.

The weeks you'd been at Clay's, there had been something. Electricity. The way Ginny looked at you when you she thought you wouldn't notice, the way she brushed her hips against yours in the cramped kitchen and played with your hair as you watched television at night, waiting for Clay to finish up in the garage, where he cut and oiled and sewed leather holsters for .45 calibers, Glocks, Berettas, long barrels. He didn't have much—a 1000-square-foot rancher, a girlfriend who read tarot at the crystal shop on Main Street, where the tourists browsed antiques and cowboy hats and dried wreaths made of chili peppers, his holsters, his crew cab—but he had everything. All you had was him.

She'd been lying in bed, sipping coffee, when you came out of the shower after your five-mile run. As you hurried between the bathroom and the open doorway of their bedroom, wrapped in a bath towel, toward your own, she'd whistled at you from the bed.

"Hey sexy," she said, and you'd stopped in your tracks, feeling goosebumps all over.

"Hey sexy yourself." It was only three words, but it was your most impressive feat so far—more than your one-handed basket at the buzzer, your game-tying free throws, your 3.8 grade point average. You sounded assured. Desirable. Changed.

"Come and talk to me." She patted Clay's side of the bed. As you slid in the sheets, you left the cocoon of your damp bath towel crumpled on the floor, pressed your Dove bodywash-smelling skin against her.

***

When Clay shows up at Roman's, three days after he threw you out, you're surprised.

"I don't know what to say." Clay shakes his head, stirring his straw in his soda as you lean over a table in the back. "I mean, what were you doing?"

"I don't know." You shake your head, too. "Ginny's been so nice to me—I guess I took it the wrong way."

"Ginny said as much." Clay nods, looking up at you. "I knew you weren't like that."

You roll a straw wrapper very tightly into a curl, not looking at him. You're not mad at Ginny for lying. You're not mad at Clay, either, for believing her. People who have things, especially if it's not many of them, spend all their time trying to not to lose them. They may want other things, but not at the expense of what they already have.

"I'm so sorry," you say after a minute. You're mad at yourself for wanting other people's things. But maybe you don't want what Clay has, anyway. There are so many ways to make families. You think of Walter and TJ, who are at the Very Large Array right now, the home of 27 radio antennas. You know the human race is wired to make contact with other planets and galaxies, other people.

"Ginny and I, we're willing to forget it," Clay says. Today, the muscles in his temples are slack, and his Bailey perfectly cradles his head. It looks good on him. "I don't know where you been staying the past week—Ginny got pretty upset when Veronica mentioned you hadn't been by—so if you want to ..."

"No." You don't want to forget who you are now. Or might be. And you're not sure you want to go back to Clay's. To school. To what you've known. Maybe you've always known that you and Clay were strangers. You think about, when you were little, the way Clay pulled you around on a sled on Christmas mornings in Wyoming. When you got to the hills behind your house, he'd carry the Radio Flyer with red metal runners over his head. At the top, you grabbed the steering bar tight as he pushed you and you started down the hill. Halfway down, you wanted to turn and look at him, wave, but you'd gained so much speed, and all you could do was hold on, see it through.

The doorbell jingles at the front of Roman's, and you jump up, as if you've been caught cheating again. It's just Javi, one of the guys who's been digging up the water main on Date Street. It's surprised you how long it'd taken for that water leak to collect below the surface, to cave in the intersection, to crumble asphalt and rock. You wonder if it can be fixed, and, if not, whether Clay and Ginny and everyone else here will stay until the bitter end, anyway.

"Where are you stayin'?" Clay grabs your forearm. You let him hold you for a second. What was once strong and comforting feels so constricting, heavy.

"It's OK—I got a place," you answer.

When Walter and TJ drive out to Las Cruces tomorrow, they'll continue onto El Paso, where they'll fly home to Portland, Oregon. But not before they put in a good word for you with Bob, the owner of the hostel. In exchange for housekeeping and covering the front desk phone when Bob run errands, he'll let you sleep in one of the bunks in the dormitory.

You break away and hurry behind the counter, grabbing the order pad, even though Javi's order is the always the same—two slices everything, a large Coke, large onion rings.

Out of the corner of your eye you watch Clay linger at the door. There's so much more that can be said, but nothing that will change your mind now. With your back turned, while you wrap Javi's slices on a plate, scoop up onion rings out of the fryer, you know Clay will go. You take your time with the onion rings, afraid to turn to face the counter, see it's only just you and Javi. And then just you, when Javi heads back up to Date Street, taking a long drink of his Coke.

***

"We'll send you a postcard," Walter says. He and TJ are standing in front of their rental Hyundai. A plastic tub of pretzels rests in the back seat like a baby. "And if you're ever in Oregon, you always have a place."

"We'll look for you on television." TJ folds his body into the front seat and slides on his aviator sunglasses. "Although what I know about basketball you can fit on my big toenail."

You wind up making a lot of friends at the hostel that last month in T or C—George and Helen from Montana, Jerri and Bobbi from Maryland. In the fall, postcards from them are forwarded to you from your old P.O. box at school to where you are now—postcards with pictures of the Chesapeake Bay, of Big Sky Country. Close to Christmas break, you get a letter from Walter, inviting you to spend a few days for the holidays. *TJ prefers the Pittock Mansion, but if you're like me, you'll dig the holiday ship parade.*

You send him a card back with your new address. And then you decide to call Clay, to let him know where you are, too. Because although there will be another Walter, another Ginny, maybe someone even better than Ginny, you will never have another brother. This information will never change.

While you wait for him to pick up, you stare in the mirror. You've never liked looking at yourself—there's so much to find fault with—but the wide, clearness of your eyes, the shape of your lips, surprises you. It's intoxicating, almost, seeing yourself from the vantage point of someone else. When Clay picks up, you say hello, but it's not really him you're greeting.

THE BOWLING STORY

The bowling story will begin and end in a bowling alley. There is a man, there is a woman, or maybe there are two couples, woman A and man B, woman C and man D. There is no baby, although one of the women may be pregnant and not know it. Maybe one woman, A, is cheating on one man, B, with the other man, D. Maybe man B finds out because the man D and woman A have placed their initials together in the high score line of the Centipede machine.

Perhaps man B just notices the alignment of particles between woman A and the man D, or maybe just the stench of beer and pheromones and gall. The other woman, C, deals with man D's infidelity by not dealing with it at all. She laughs and jokes with man B, who is tense. Maybe she notices his long-suffering shoulders. Maybe she is attracted to them. Maybe she is repulsed by them. Maybe she goes into the ladies room and lights a cigarette, even though she quit three months ago.

The couples live in upstate New York. Everyone who is having a literary epiphany in a bowling alley lives in upstate New York. It is winter. The dormancy of the landscape should be emphasized. The careening of pins, the fuzz of seventies album-oriented rock on the speaker system, the blip-blip-blip of Centipede, the dull roll of bowling balls should all represent the inner friction of each subject.

***

Duckpin bowling is said to have been invented at the turn of the twentieth century by a couple of baseball players from the Baltimore Orioles who wanted a lane above their favorite bar. However, because the ceiling upstairs was low, the room cramped, smaller balls and pins were introduced. The pins, when knocked over, were said to look like a bunch of geese flying, hence duckpins. In 1982, when I was ten, I bowled in a duckpin league in Baltimore. I inherited my bowling balls from a relative who gave up bowling like it was bad habit. One ball was baby blue swirled and the other was pink swirled. They lived in a periwinkle blue and white bowling bag. After I became too cool for bowling, I bequeathed them to my grandmother, who had begun bowling in a senior duckpin league. When she died, we all wanted things from her. Everybody wanted jewelry or her Bible or her photos. I didn't want my bowling balls back at the time. I wanted my grandmother's scents, the smell of chicken a la king and coffee. I wanted the sounds of the back screen door creaking shut, her soft gutteral laugh. How does one begin to look for such things? For bowling balls?

***

The two couples in the bowling story, however, will use balls issued by the bowling alley. They're not a team, not serious bowlers. They come once, maybe a few times, for a lack of anything better to do. It's a town in upstate New York with not much to offer. The couples are stir-crazy, trapped. They are probably Brooklyn transplants teaching at SUNY-Buffalo. Trapped in this town, in these relationships. There will be some subtly crafted paragraph alluding to how the events in our lives are just bowling balls careening toward us, how we will get knocked down and stacked up over and over and, in all, one strike will mean nothing more to the pins than a gutter ball. There will be some subtle reference to the futility of it, the existential despair, and then grudging acceptance.

Man B, who is tense, has had too much beer, and woman A has taken his keys. He bumps into her, tells her he's not drunk and that maybe she just wants to ride home with her lover boy D. There is some pushing between the men. Woman C who doesn't deal with things shouts at them to finish the frame. She is winning and fears this victory will elude her. Woman A walks away from group and heads over to the Centipede machine, where she fishes a quarter from her pocket and begins to play. It is man B's turn to bowl. But instead of stepping onto the lane, he goes to the Centipede machine.

You never take me seriously, he says to her.

It is a particularly critical point in the video game. The mushrooms that the centipede weaves through are built up heavily, making a tunnel down to the bottom of the screen. But because the centipede is trapped in the tunnel, the shooter can kill most of the centipede before it can make its escape.

The rollerball is spinning wildly under woman A's hand. Man B has had too much to drink. He heaves the bowling ball upward and then down onto the video screen. The video screen shatters and shorts. Woman A falls back. The bowling alley is silent for a moment, silent of human sound and energy, a still frame, before woman A runs back to man D, who is trying to make good with woman C, rubbing her shoulders and complementing her on a great game. Man B, meanwhile, feels the bottom dropping out of him somewhere. He is the drain and the events of tonight and the day before and the year before swirl through him before the manager comes over, his face red and meaty like corned beef, and tells him he's going to pay for that machine, he's going to pay, buddy, fucking drunk.

Woman C, who is winning, knows they will not finish the game. She stuffs the score sheet in her purse and slips outside, tapping out a Virginia Slims from the pack she's been hiding from man D. It's dark but the snow everywhere makes the sky soft, purple. The metaphor here is of some sort of purgatory. There will be a bookmark caught in a tree branch. Woman C takes it as a sign, some Sisyphus sort of irony about her life, when a pleasant-looking man she had noticed earlier comes out with his black bowling bag. Although he bowled with a team, on the league side of the alley, she noticed him here and there, keeping to himself. He happens upon her reaching in vain for the bookmark when he, notably taller, plucks it from the tree and presents it to her. She opens her mouth to thank him but he leaves without a word. She stands in the purple-white quiet, holding the bookmark and cigarette. She does not want to go back inside. She does not know yet that she is pregnant.

***

My favorite memory of bowling at the American Fairlanes on Eastern Avenue in Baltimore is a bookmark caught in a tree branch just outside the doors on a windy day. My mother and I, avid readers, both coveted the bookmark but were too short to reach it.

Just then, the brother and sister came outside. Brother and sister were older than I. They were probably sixteen or seventeen and were quiet, annihilating bowlers with super high averages. I used to marvel at the size of brother's feet, his long bangs and cratered face, his giant's height (in retrospect, probably six feet). Brother and sister were a gritty, unsmiling Keith and Laurie Partridge (later, Thurston Moore and Kim Gordon, when I discovered indie rock). I considered brother and sister wise back then, although now I probably consider them lower middle class, dim, driving Pontiacs.

Brother and sister were walking past my mother, who was reaching in vain for the plastic tasseled bookmark with Garfield or Cathy or some other popular 1980s icon, when brother stopped, plucked the bookmark out of the tree, and handed it to my mother.

My mother and I both wanted to marry brother that day. The American Fairlanes on Eastern Avenue closed on April 30, 2009. I wonder if brother and sister still bowl. I wonder who is in possession of their bowling balls, how I can obtain them. They are just as much a part of my memories as theirs, and I thereby claim some right to them.

***

This is where the bowling story will end, with woman C outside holding the bookmark. Of course, it will not end there. The man A and woman B by the Centipede machine will probably break up, and the couples will never go back to the bowling alley. It may be awkward on campus for a while. Man D and woman C may or may not have a baby together. Maybe one of the men or women accepts a teaching position somewhere else, and the particular nucleus of this group is degraded, back to its core elements, like hydrogen and oxygen.

One person will try and remember who introduced everyone to each other. Everyone else will try to forget.

The owner of the bowling alley gets rid of the Centipede machine, rather than repairing it, and then, there is one less forward-thinking rollerball console video game in the world. After a while, a children's prize machine appears in its place. It sells light-up yo-yos and pencil tops, all matter of ticky-tack. Things of no value that, when we are young and know no better, we hold dear to our hearts.

THE PIANO

X. bought the upright 1881 Steinway for two thousand dollars from a second-hand store a few blocks over from Washington University. She had been intending to look at a 19th-century English mahogany Chippendale ribbon back settee she had seen in the storefront on her way to work, a perfect addition, she felt, to her front hallway. All morning, during her pediatric rounds, she felt the weight and angles of the settee graze the inside of her skull, presenting a fine argument of classic ornamentation much needed in her recently purchased townhouse, still shiny with Windex and Pine Sol and soft, velvety moving boxes that sharply divided her life from Y's. But when she walked through the dark, musty store, her hospital clogs sinking into the nuzzled warmness of the old, Oriental rug lining the path from door to register, she came upon it, the Steinway, pressed between the stairwell leading to the second floor and a mauve French Empire sofa whose cushions were littered with sheet music.

How Y. would have loved this, she thought, quite unexpectedly, for she had given up all thoughts of what Y had wanted months ago. It was all quite academic, she had wanted to believe. She had accepted a fellowship in Pediatrics at Washington University just as Y. had decided to remain teaching music theory at Rutgers, living in Trenton, close to Y's ailing mother. It was a divorce without the tears, at least for X. A handshake, a dividing of the assets from their four years together, with Y. keeping most of the contemporary furniture that X. hated anyway. It had happened so fast, the breakup, and not with much of X's attention. Instead, X. flew back and forth to St. Louis, looking at homes near the university, filling out forms, changing her mailing address and proper identity on the hundreds of small items that somehow named and identified her.

There was simply no room for reflection. And now, she thought, months later, there was simply no place for it. But with the dull ebony finish of the Steinway, the elaborate cutaway backdrop, the yellowed ivory keys, the instrument begged for love and restoration.

"It needs some work. You'll definitely want to get new strings." The Ukrainian woman, round and plump and moving in short waves while stationary, explained when X. inquired about the price. "But the soundboard and bridges are intact. That's rare for a piano this old, one that hasn't been restored. It has good tone, too. Do you play?"

"Not at all," X. admitted, somewhat embarrassed. "I just think it's beautiful."

"Ah, you should take lessons." The old woman gathered up the sheet music and dropped herself softly onto the piano bench. "You're going to get a lot of enjoyment out of this piano."

X. watched the old woman put on her glasses, which were chained around her neck with an odd assortment of brownish glass beads, and played what X. recognized as a waltz. The old woman's hands strained to reach the keys, her bones trapped under long tarps of wrinkled, spotted flesh. The sound was not good, that X. could tell, even as the woman played measured and delicately for half a minute. X. wondered what she was doing. She had not decided to buy the piano to lure Y. to St. Louis, or even to remember Y. And yet this piano presented a piece, perhaps, the last piece to a puzzle she wanted to admire briefly before breaking it apart and funneling it back into the box.

***

When it was delivered at ten o'clock the next Saturday, X. asked the piano movers if they wanted some tea.

"It's a fine instrument, and we'd love to have tea and hear you play it, but we gotta run," the older man, the one who did the speaking, explained, dabbing his face with a soiled handkerchief.

"Are you sure? Perhaps one of you plays?" She took a few steps toward the piano, where it rested beneath a Kandinsky print in the front room with the bay window.

"You don't play?" The younger man, who had a peach-fuzz head, face covered with acne, asked.

"Well, no," X. said, only now realizing the full responsibility of her ownership.

The younger man took a step toward the piano as X. extended her hand. He wiped the seat of his uniform and sat on the bench.

"I took lessons when I was little...don't remember shit," he laughed, his fingers hovering above the keys. "I can play chopsticks, though."

He pushed his long, thin fingers onto the keys, making the room hum softly with staccato. The older man laughed as he folded the order requisition and shoved it into his front pocket.

"Don't quit your day job, maestro," he said. X. stood by the window, watching them as they pulled away from the curb. She turned to stare at the Steinway, arms crossed. She felt as if a baby had been left on her doorstep, and she wondered whether she should call someone and have it inspected, given a full physical.

X. had not cared much about pianos, at least the nuts and bolts of them. Y. had a respectable Apollo at the house they shared in Trenton that only needed the occasional tuning for it to interpret respectable Chopin sonatas through the inquiry of Y's fingers. For X., music was a pleasant thing heard at the grocery store or reception area. She did not understand what Y. meant when she spoke of the intricacies of organization, time keys, signatures, harmonies, accidentals, or even of feeling certain chord progressions tickle the back of one's neck.

And now, X. could not even appreciate the simple pleasure of background noise, for she could not play. She sat at the bench and looked at the keys, depressing one here and here, listening to the soft gasps of noise that vibrated from the strings inside the Steinway. She tumbled a few notes together; they sounded like little coughs, a disease she was uncertain of curing. She ran her hand instead over the smooth ebony finish, reminding her of her pediatric patients, bubbled cherubs who had not been pulled like taffy into their angled adulthood.

She looked up restorers in the yellow pages when she got home from work that week, left messages, got estimates, and yet she knew for all this restoration, she could not make the piano play. She had decided against lessons the first evening her visitor settled into her home; she blamed it on scheduling, a lack of time resulting from her sixty-hour workweeks at the hospital. But she knew it was more than that. She was not a musician.

She would need to find others. She had a cocktail party, some colleagues from her department, sipping chardonnay and eating cheese and crackers while the soft murmur of conversations filled the living room. But the conversations always turned to the same question; did she play?

"My ex was a pianist, a professor. I guess I was used to having one in the house, even if I never touched it," she laughed, explaining to an internist whose thick dark hair was close enough to touch. "It's kind of like dating an artist and just collecting art, no?"

The wife of another fellow sat down at the piano and played *Greensleeves*. The notes came from deep within, slightly muffled, as if struggling with emphysema. X's guests listened politely, as the fellow's wife pressed onto the yellowed ivory keys in inquiry. X. wondered whether it was too late to trade the Steinway for the Chippendale.

"It needs a little work," she explained later, after several guests had tried bits of Rachmaninoff and Bach, Gershwin. "I've been getting restoration estimates. I think it makes a nice decorative piece, at any rate."

When X. noted her cleaning lady eyeing the piano the next week, she implored her to play.

"Well, I can play a little bit, you know—my husband likes show tunes," she explained, but then looked at her grubby pink t-shirt with roses and faded denim jeans. "But I bet that cost you a fortune."

"Not really," X lied. "And I bought it to be played." She extended her hand toward the bench and sat on the Napoleon III-style sofa while the cleaning lady pounded out a song from *Guys and Dolls*, her small body bouncing off the bench as she wrestled with the soft keys and whispering, breathless notes. X. remembered Y's long, slender body, wrapped in a kimono, playing etudes in the evening in Trenton while X. drove her eyes into medical journals on the other side of the room. She tried to remember the serene expression, the soft long line of Y's lips as she glided up and down the keys effortlessly, as if she were undertaking a morning stretch. She tried to imagine Y. at this instrument, what seduction would have to occur to make the notes sound vital, confident, alive.

"Bravo." X. leaned forward and clapped as the cleaning lady leaned back and caught her breath. "I didn't realize you were so talented."

"Thanks, ma'am." The cleaning lady stood up, her skin shades of pink to match her t-shirt. "I'd better get going. These houses don't clean themselves."

"Feel free to play at any time," X. said at the door as the cleaning lady left, vacuum tumbling behind her like a petulant child. She thought briefly, very briefly, of having the piano delivered to the cleaning lady's house, where at least some Rodgers and Hammerstein could be enjoyed by the masses, but knew the restoration might be prohibitive for a cleaning lady and her electrician husband. She also knew that the black burden sitting in her townhouse, and yes, it had begun to feel that way, for reasons she could not quite articulate, was hers and hers alone. She had to restore it to its former glory, make it sing, somehow.

The idea occurred to her at night. For many days, she wrote it off as a nocturnal delusion. For who would spend two thousand dollars on a piano only to do *that* to it? But it plagued her, plagued her during rounds, during consultations, during martinis after dinner with colleagues, and on the treadmill at the hospital gym. Perhaps it plagued her longer in her life, how to get to the heart of something so foreign, a talent seemingly out of her skill set, how to approach something she was so unaccustomed to wanting or needing and yet she knew brought so much joy, so much careless happiness to others. And it would be all in the approach she, as a surgeon, knew.

X. approached the instrument cautiously. Perhaps it only needed conservative surgery. She opened it up and looked at the row of strings inside. Carefully, she removed two of them, then played the corresponding keys. A soft clink chirped from them. She took the wires and hung them outside her kitchen window. The long, tangling cords looked like mutant daddy longlegs tickling the glass.

The surgery became more extensive. She then got a screwdriver and began popping up some of the yellowed ivories, leaving the piano looking like a prizefighter. She leaned a few keys against the terra cotta bricks in her garden, a few on the outside window sill of her bedroom. She removed one of the pedals and replaced her doorknocker with it. She placed the backdrop with the soft cloth lining outside her back door, strapped to the railing to catch a breeze through the cloth. She placed a few ebony keys in the birdfeeder, left some on the floor for the cat to bat around.

Then, after a week of letting the instrument acclimate to its new configuration, she began to listen. At first, there was silence. She listened harder, so much so that she forgot to breathe. Gradually, she began to breathe quietly and close her eyes, quiet her mind. She began to hear the rain plunking against the ivories in the garden, the wind blowing softly through the cloth in the cutout backdrop, the piano wires scraping against the glass during breezy evenings, a woodpecker drilling through one of the ebony keys, others being scooted across the floor in compulsion by a furry black paw. Underneath all these things was a metronome that someone had placed expertly, without X.'s knowledge, in the folds of her chest, drawing them together, in concert between air and space.

THE GOODBYE PARTY

Alvin said he wanted to go to the goodbye party with Sam. They were on the subway coming home from Alvin's school. Alvin wore the straps of his child-sized backpack around his ankles, the pouch part resting atop his outstretched legs. Sam had always told him not to do that, that they needed to get up and off the subway car quickly, but what Alvin said about the goodbye party stunned Sam into silence, and when the car braked at their station, he lifted Alvin over his shoulder and ferried him off, backpack hanging from Alvin's legs.

He had not told Alvin about the goodbye parties, believing he was not ready to understand. Alvin had barely understood his mother's death almost a year ago, although now and then he displayed such surprising resoluteness and peace about it that it had aged him, had made Sam feel like the child, crying while making a peppered-turkey sandwich in the kitchen because he had gotten the turkey from the deli Elizabeth loved.

But last Saturday, when Alvin had gotten up in the middle of the night, a bad dream, and found that Sam wasn't home, he had asked his grandmother, who was babysitting, where his father was. Sam's mother, not sure what answer would be acceptable to Alvin, and very annoyed at Sam for not accounting for this scenario—but only slightly so that she had not accounted for it—said to wait until his father got home.

It was a goodbye party for the dogs at the shelter, Sam had explained later that morning, eyes still wet, a burn in his left shoulder from cradling an 80-pound Rottweiler, Mugsy, whose eyes were root-beer candies, as the shelter employees had arrived. A goodbye party because they're getting adopted.

Alvin, still in bed, wearing his Hulk pajamas, had patted Sam's head where he crouched near the pillow, smelling the sweet-sour of his son's sleep.

It had been enough for Alvin at the time. There had been no follow-up questions, why the goodbye party was on a Saturday night, lasted all night, why he hadn't been informed of them before. Perhaps after his mother became an angel he believed that there was nothing left to know, or perhaps he felt that the most important question of his boyhood had been answered so unsatisfyingly that he could not trust his father for answers to anything else.

They got home from the subway station, Sam breathing a sigh of relief. They had talked on the walk back to the apartment about an art project Alvin's class had begun that day: painting the seasons. Alvin explained in great detail the objects he had chosen to represent summer: a shovel and pail for the beach, his BMX-style bicycle, his sunglasses and suntan lotion, the sun, green trees, squiggly lines that represented the Mid-Atlantic summer heat, and a dog with a long pink tongue. Because dogs pant when it's hot, Alvin explained.

But he had not continued about the goodbye party, nor had he taken the opportunity to ask Sam whether they could get a dog, the latter because he knew the landlord's policy of no dogs. The apartment, a cramped four rooms on the second floor of an old gingerbread Victorian that needed repainting, could not even tolerate a cat, with its hardwood floors, banister, and window panes that were drafty in the winter.

It was not until the next day at dinner that Alvin brought it up again.

Can I go to the goodbye party if I can't get a dog? He looked up at Sam from the chicken and rice and cheese scrambled on his plate to resemble a casserole.

I'll think about it, Sam answered. The night before, Sam had thought about how to explain the parties. He had not even told his mother about them at first, saying instead he was going out for dinner and drinks with Jeff and Maria from college and would not be back until late. He thought she would think he was disturbed, that he needed to go back to therapy and really work through Elizabeth's death, along with the transition to being Alvin's primary caregiver while working full time at home, taking Alvin to the Montessori school in the morning and picking him up, remembering his vaccinations, making sure to get the right kind of frankfurter pasta for Alvin's lunches and pediatric cough medicine while waking up every morning to the same essential truth, that he was a widower and his son would grow up without his mother. And Elizabeth, who knows what she saw from wherever she was and what she would miss?

He'd read about the goodbye parties during a visit to the dentist in a newsletter that the local shelter put out. He'd called the shelter to see if the parties were still held and explained his situation. He needed this, he had told them, although he did not know why. His mother would say he was sticking his finger in an open wound, the way he did when he was a little boy, poking at the pink tissue glistening with blood, feeling the mettle of his parts, amazed that he was not made of steel, or, like his sister's Barbie dolls, a hard rubber with bolts. But he thought it was more like picking a scab, which he had also done back in those days, impatient for the healing process to complete and, he thought, helping it along.

The first party had been terrible for Sam. The dogs, mostly large, dangerous-seeming breeds like Rottweilers and Pit Bulls and mutts of the former, were clear-eyed and regal, all muscle and graceful arches of back and gut, compact behinds, lively, whipped tails, and delicate paws with trimmed nails. They licked his face when he clung to them and cried. They opened their snouts and closed them, as if to say, hey, it's our goodbye party, not yours. That morning he had waited at the station for the train to start running again, his head low, body shaking, and he understood why people killed, why people stopped feeling, why people stopped believing in God. He heard the first train of the day burrowing through the tunnel to his hub, and he thought of throwing himself on the tracks. But then he thought of his mother, his sister, Alvin, Elizabeth, and knew that giving love to the world was more important than the pain it gave you.

Still, he hadn't planned on going back to the shelter. But one of the other volunteers, Tim, an AIDs survivor, had called him up to see whether he was coming. *I was just like you the first time,* Tim said. *But it gets better. Not that it ain't hard still.*

He had not asked Tim or Alicia, the volunteer coordinator, whether it would be all right if he could bring Alvin to the next goodbye party. But he thought, if Alvin asked again, he would take him. After all, Elizabeth had died and Alvin still went to first grade and painted spring, summer, fall, and winter. He looked at the free flyers from Target and Toys 'R Us that arrived in the mail and noted with glee the availability of the newest cartridge for his hand-held video game system. He loved trains, and not the preschool cartoon ones¾all manner of steam engines, cabooses, hopper cars, and box cars lined the shelves of his room. He had developed into a boy without his mother, who would develop into a teenager and become interested in girls (or boys) and maybe skateboarding or football or sketching. He would go to college, Sam hoped. The goodbye party would not push Alvin off course, leaving him clinging to a life vest and flotsam in the sea of his development.

Of course, Alicia may not see it that way, may call social services. It seemed that, for a few months after Elizabeth's death, Sam and Alvin had lived in a world of made-up rules, rules that worked for them. Macaroni for breakfast. Watching Spongebob DVDs at four in the morning. Camping in the backyard in the snow. But others had encroached on them, Sam's mother when Alvin came to her house in a pajama top, jeans, and beach sandals instead of proper fall attire, Alvin's teachers when he brought his mother's death certificate in for show-and-tell and talked about what happens at a funeral. After that, Sam was afraid that the next time they strayed off the path of structure and eight-o'clock bedtimes and no hooky from work/school to conquer Super Mario world, Alvin would be taken from him, whisked to a world where he paid for Elizabeth's death over and over, with strangers and their pity and siblings who played with him gently because they thought he would break.

Sam did not tell his mother, nor did he tell the shelter. The Saturday afternoon before his shift, he kept his cell phone in his hand for hours, ready to call his mother and arrange for emergency babysitting. Alvin played in the yard with a balsa wood airplane he had made in art class the day before. He had taken some of his trains outside and lined them on the ground, attacked them with the airplane. Sam tried not to read too much into it. All boys killed things with their fingers, with their cars and trucks, in their drawings. Even Sam still played first-person shooter games on his laptop.

But he wondered what Alvin would get from the goodbye party. Surely not the same things he had¾the feeling of being in the moment in the face of inevitable loss, of enjoying the dog thoroughly, its fur, its eyes, its teeth, the gait of its walk, its favorite toy and treat. To enjoy themselves together despite it, despite the light purple, then pink, then yellow of the dawn filling the windows in the kennels, a light that burned out the last few seconds, exposing the film, melting the celluloid, and leaving the theater screen white.

He had had moments like these with Elizabeth, a book of Margaret Atwood poems he read to her at hospice, a surprise thunderstorm that they had watched from her bed, holding hands. While looking through pictures of their honeymoon in St. Petersburg, back when the journey of their life had felt long and relaxed, easy like their elbows and knees and smiles. And so had Alvin, if only because every child experiences time without a past or a future. And he hoped that Alvin still lived in this disjointed way, present after present, even after he went to the goodbye party.

They had dinner, spaghetti and meatballs with extra Parmesan for Alvin, the top of his noodles looking like sawdust. Sam had a bottle of Stella Artois. They listened to an old Chet Baker record. Then, when it was time for Alvin's bath, Sam squatted beside him, hands on Alvin's shoulders.

Guess what? I've got a surprise for you tonight. We're going to the goodbye party.

Alvin sat with Sam on the train, swinging his legs. Sam studied him carefully. Mostly he beamed, proud of his inclusion in a very grownup event, something that extended well past his bedtime, although something he could not talk about at show and tell the next week. (Sam had already made him cross his heart/double promise). But a few times, it seemed as if Alvin frowned, or looked worried, although it could have been any number of things, the way the train picked up speed and jolted to a stop between the second and third station, the fact it was past his bedtime (Sam planned to leave the goodbye party early tonight), the extra serving of meatballs in his small stomach. Sam squeezed Alvin's hand, small and clammy, and he tried to be present with its size and heft, noting tomorrow it would be different, that it would already have grown out of tonight's size and heft, nothing left but the memory.

The shelter was behind a sporting stadium. Sometimes the volunteers brought some of the dogs to the sporting events for adoption and to drum up publicity for the shelter. But mostly, people didn't know about it. It looked like an average concrete warehouse with a nine-foot barbed wire fence surrounding the back, which was filled with dirt and balls and a few chewed-over toys.

Will there be cake? Alvin asked as they walked up to the doors. How come we didn't bring any gifts?

We'll be giving the dogs a gift, Sam answered. You'll see.

At first, Sam was ashamed. Ashamed of the way the shelter smelled, like feces and urine and kibble, and how it looked, with beige-painted cinderblock walls that held antibacterial hand lotion carrels on every wall, the cracked concrete floor, the continual barking of dogs who were confused, lonely, irritated, and scared. But he realized that Alvin probably did not notice any of these things. He had already broken free of Sam's hand and leaned on tip-toe to look through the glass window of the door leading to the kennels. Alicia, who was in her forties, who wore her graying hair in a loose bun and whose eyebrows seemed continually furrowed, strode up to Sam.

That's my son, Alvin. Sam began first, before she could speak. He has asked me for weeks to come to the goodbye parties. He just wants to pet the dogs, play with them for a little bit, and then we'll go home.

I don't know, Sam, Alicia said, straightening her cat's eye glasses. I'm going to have to call Ed about this. There may be liability issues.

Like what? No one has to know we're here. Come on, Alicia. It's only for a few hours.

Sam, don't put me in this position...

Let us go in for a few minutes. You can tell them I left something here last time and I came to pick it up. Or that I couldn't get babysitting tonight and stopped by to tell you because my phone died. I don't know¾you're a smart lady, Alicia. You'll figure something out and let us do this.

Jesus, you put me in a bad spot, Sam. Jesus...five minutes, okay? She looked at the signup clipboard in her hand. Only because it's so hard to get volunteers...and I don't want to lose you.

Thanks. He squeezed her shoulder, found that he enjoyed touching her. I owe you a coffee.

They walked past the kennels into another room, where five dogs sniffed around, mingling with Tim and Ly, an older Vietnamese widow who had lost her twelve-year-old Mastiff that year and could not afford the physical and financial commitment of a new dog.

Son? She pointed at Alvin, who had already taken an interest in a Border Collie mix that lay on its belly.

Yes, Sam answered. He wanted to come play with the dogs.

He don't know, right? She shook her head. What happens to them?

No...he thinks it's like a birthday party, Sam answered. He felt suddenly sick. At what point would he tell Alvin? He could not wait ten years, or even tell him when they got home. He should have already told him, well before tonight. He wondered if Alicia was calling child protective services as they spoke.

The approach had been different for Elizabeth's illness. They'd taken Alvin to Dave and Busters. Elizabeth had already been through surgery and radiation and chemo and walked with a cane. A wheelchair laid flat in the trunk of the Subaru for emergencies. Her hair had grown back but she was still bat-like, angled with visible ribs above her breasts and ears that stuck out through short tufts of hair. After a night of basketball hoops and video games and buzzers and bleeps that created its own cloud of anesthetic gas, they'd driven home, given Alvin a bath, and after reading his favorite book at bedtime, they sat on his bed and told him about the angels that come to take people to heaven, including his mother.

It had taken a few days after the angel talk for the questions. Then, a week later, Alvin had become angry. Can't we share mommy? He had asked Sam one night in the Arby's drive-thru. Why do the angels get to have her the whole time?

Because some people are so special, so important, that when the angels need them, they have to go. It's an honor, really. Think about being so good, so important, Alvin, that you got all the gold stars in your class...every single one of them. That's what Mommy is like to those angels. Sam thought it was a good answer, but he knew how Alvin felt, how angry, and he was afraid to tell him he was angry, too.

This is the one I want, Daddy. Alvin held the Border Collie mix in a headlock. It shook its black head, salted with white, and grinned at Sam, brown eyes like wood stain, its tongue pebbled with saliva. Sam picked up a tennis ball, soggy, balding, as the dog tracked it with his eyes, all business now. Sam rolled it across the room like a bowling ball, and the dog burst out of Alvin's grasp, its legs pistons under its thick fur, toenails scrabbling across the concrete. Alvin laughed as the dog returned, ball in mouth, and dared Sam to extract it from his death grip.

Sam imagined this dog in their cramped apartment. It could sleep on the sofa during the day, or even follow the panes of light across the living room floor, ending up in the kitchen. Or he could sleep at Sam's feet while he worked. They could take a long walk at lunch, and then after dinner, with Alvin. The landlord wouldn't have to know, or the neighbors. They could even move, if it came to that.

Give him a treat. Ly held the plastic barrel of dog biscuits out to Alvin, who reached his hand in like Halloween, pulling out three or four, green and tan and red ones. The dog dropped the ball and sat before him at attention. It was hard to believe this dog, a perfectly wonderful, obedient dog, was at the goodbye party. It was so hard to believe any of them were. Sam looked over at Tim, who wrestled with two dogs, one a shepherd mix, the other an indeterminate mutt. They hooked their paws over his forearms and barked, nudging their heads, little boulders, into his chest when he stopped for a breath.

Ly tried to get a wheat-colored pit bull with a pink eraser nose to earn a treat. Sit. She made a stern face at him. Roll over. Roll over. Sit.

Tim opened the door to the outside run, and all the dogs filed out into the night, their gait leisurely, sniffing the corners of the fences near the weeds. They had been outside in the run plenty of times, Sam imagined, but this was probably the first time at night. If they were superstitious at all, distrustful, they did not show it. Tomorrow, other dogs would fill the run, some of them just surrendered or found, and smell these dogs, the scent of their calling, and wonder where they were, where they had gone.

I like Charlie. Alvin came up to Sam where he sat at the picnic table and he whipped his arms waist high like he did when his favorite cartoon came on Saturday mornings or when they went to the zoo. The Border Collie padded over to them with the tennis ball, and Sam wrestled it from his jaws. He could smell traces of the dog shampoo they used to clean the animals when they came into the shelter. He wondered if he would smell it on his fingers later.

Charlie, huh? You like old Charlie? Sam craned his head, looking for Alicia, who had not come out into the run. He asked Ly to keep an eye on Alvin and went back into the shelter, where Alicia sat at a metal desk doing paperwork.

Thanks again for letting us come. He sat on the vinyl seat across the desk. He imagined that the adoptions also happened here, since there was a file cabinet and a shelf on which rested bundles of adoption care packages.

Just don't ask again, huh? She eyed him, not moving her head from her work.

Listen...my boy really likes that Border Collie mix. You think we can put a hold on him?

Sam, you told me your apartment situation doesn't allow pets. Alicia leaned back in her chair. It moaned between them.

We could move. I've been looking for a place closer to my mother, anyway. He rolled a pencil, green painted and chewed, by human or canine he did not know, across the desk calendar. He seems really well behaved, very gentle with the ball.

Sam, don't. She reached across the desk and slid her hand over his. When he looked up at her, she pulled it away, resting her palm, fingers spread, on the pile of papers. Sam, I would love to adopt all of these dogs tonight, but I can't. And you, if you were serious, you would have to come back tomorrow right when the shelter opens and put in an application and we would reject it because I know you lied about your living situation.

But it'll keep the dog alive a little longer, won't it? And who knows, maybe I will have signed a lease by the end of the week. Or maybe someone else will come.

He and Elizabeth had begun, in the end, to make plans using the date "a little longer." If Elizabeth could hang on a little longer, they could possibly find a new trial to enter. They were always starting new trials at the NIH. Alvin's birthday was only three months away; Sam's five. It she held on a little longer, they might be able to celebrate Halloween.

Sam, you're a good guy, said Alicia. If you could have a dog, you would already have one or two. And even though you can't give a dog a home right now, you're doing the best you can for these dogs, to make sure their last memory is happy.

Alicia, I can do this. Sam leaned in. The pencil shook, and when he dropped the pencil, his hands were shaking. I want that dog to have a happy ending.

Sam, let me know when your situation changes. She stood up. We'll have a great dog for you. She walked toward the door and looked out into the run, and Sam was inclined to follow. He felt light-headed and wished there was a way someone could pick them up, his mother, anyone. He would sit in the back seat, face pressed against the brushed velour of the seat, and watch the night trees race with the moon, the car going and going until Sam fell asleep.

Outside, Ly and Alvin were sitting together at the picnic table, petting their dogs. She explained to Alvin, with the motion of her hand, how dogs like to be petted. Her dog licked her hand over and over, and she laughed. He wondered if she had been alone with her Mastiff when it died, how long she had waited to have it picked up, whether she tried to do it herself. Whether she lay on the bed and stroked the numb flesh and fur until her own flesh and organs had also numbed, and what she did when the numbness had begun to thaw.

It was good to see you and Sam tonight. Alicia turned to him slightly, arms crossed. I'll see you next month, okay?

Sam walked out into the run, waved at Alvin. Alvin, we've got to go. Say goodbye to Charlie.

But I want Charlie to come home with us. Alvin's face had begun to redden, his body overtaken by the same shaking as Sam's.

Come on, buddy. Sam enveloped him with his arms, his body, so that Alvin could see nothing but him, his plaid shirt, smell his cologne, feel the knot of chest hair that sprung from the base of his neck. You know the apartment rules.

Can we come see Charlie next week? Alvin asked into Sam's shoulder. Or will he be adopted then?

***

Sam sprung for a cab back to their apartment. Once they got there, they went to the Friendly's at the shopping center a little ways down the road. Even though it was breakfast, they ordered two Happy Ending sundaes.

Alvin, we have to talk about the goodbye parties. Sam patted his hands dry with his napkin as Alvin, long spoon in his little fist, plunged it into the whipped cream of his sundae.

Can dogs eat sundaes? Alvin asked.

I don't know, he answered. I guess.

It's too bad we can't share with Charlie. I wouldn't want a goodbye party without sundaes.

When Elizabeth had died, there had been no goodbye. He had woken up in the morning in the chair in her hospice room and she had not.

Here, Daddy. Alvin leaned over the table with a heaping of his sundae, ready to slide off his spoon. Eat it. It's a goodbye party.

Sam opened his mouth. The nerves in his gums screamed, not ready for the cold.

THE CLUB OF THE
MISSING

What you learn: It is so easy to disappear.

What you discover about the tip line: that everyone looks like someone in this world. Everyone buys a bag of potato chips in the Piggly Wiggly at four in the afternoon after school and exits the store but some make it home and some do not but everyone has seen that girl or boy, every mimic of them in every state, and leaves a message. And some have never seen them but claim they have, lie about the details because they too are lost and have a need to belong to something.

Did you try sonar? the woman who has developed a liking for police-station coffee will ask. There are groups for everything: divorce, disease, death. She carries a manila folder to every meeting, its spine arched, fat, edges velvety, a sudoku of phone numbers, case reports, and badge numbers written across, a name on top. *The divers can only dive so far.*

So far the rescue can stretch, the bloodhounds can sniff, the helicopter can fly. So long the flyers can hang before disintegrating. So long the parties assemble with flashlights and hiking poles and theories. *I think they've, like, finished their mission here.* Jesus boy wipes his lips and caps his Nalgene bottle. *They just vaporize into soul frequency. They just vanish into thin air.*

What also vanishes: bowling leagues, book clubs. Sunday brunch and Saturday ballet. Weeks, months, years. The exact location of a mole, a laugh line. The sound of a voice.

False starts: a wallet in the weeds, corpse-like shadows in coves where waves hackle through the water, bite the sand, and lurch away. Security footage, grainy syncopating bodies, sped up, slowed down, backward, forward. There and then not. There and not.

Every morning, a new private message on the Facebook page. A pause before every click, a breath of resolve, wondering what this day will dangle, then snatch away.

ARE YOU READY TO BE HEARTBROKEN?

Jonas wonders when the fireworks will start, how close it is to midnight. It feels like he walked outside of Mark's New Year's party hours ago, but it's probably just the beer, the case of opened Straub near his feet, that is expanding and contracting the hours and minutes in his mind. The bonfire, echoing his condition, ebbs low before roaring to twice its size.

"You avoiding me?"

Jonah looks down into the mouth of his beer, thinking it's his wife speaking. When he looks up, though, it's Julia, Mark's sister. She lights a cigarette, leaning over the deck and looking down at him. A white plume of smoke rises upward into the darkness from her lips, cloaking her face for a minute. When it disappears, she's smirking at him.

"Are you?" She's wearing one of Mark's lined flannel shirts, the one he used to wear snowboarding in the Poconos, and on Julia it looks like a wool trash bag. He watches her bound down the stairs of the deck in oversized duck boots, also Mark's—she'd flown in for the holidays from LA and apparently either greatly underestimated the cold front that had been predicted or just hadn't cared.

"Of course not—I didn't even know you were here," he says when she joins him by the fire. He pulls a pack of cigarettes out of the pocket of Mark's flannel shirt and fingers out a cigarette. "How long are you in town?"

"I don't know. Mark said I could stay as long as I wanted, but I don't know if I'm feeling the East coast vibe." Her hair, the color of a dirty penny, flows out from Mark's Philadelphia Eagles skullcap. "Or my brother."

"But you're wearing all his clothes," Jonas answers. "Isn't that kind of feeling him?"

"You're such a fucking dork," she laughs. "How're Karen and Mia?"

"Karen's inside, Mia's at a friend's," Jonas answers, lighting the cigarette. He'll get shit later from Karen about smoking, he's sure. They stand in silence for a minute, maybe more, the fire crackling. Jonas' cheeks burn, but he stays next to Julia.

"I heard your dad died," she says finally. "I'm sorry."

"It was a long time coming," he answers. "But thanks."

"Mark said he had some cabin in Bedford or something." She flicks her cigarette into the bonfire.

"Yeah." He rubs the side of his neck, the stubble almost electric on his palm. "I guess we'll keep it for vacations or something, although Karen wants to sell it, use the money for Mia's college."

He had wanted to go to the cabin for New Year's Eve, the three of them, some familial orbit, one that they'd all been drifting in and out of for some time. But Mia had insisted on spending the night at a friend's house. A girl they hadn't even met. *I don't even like pot*, Dad, Mia had preempted his speech about sleepovers a few days before at dinner.

"How old's Mia now?" Julia taps out another cigarette, glancing back at the house.

"Thirteen—can you believe it?" Jonas smiles. "She's as old as you were when I went off to college."

"You were always so nice to me." Julia glances at him, wrapping her arms around herself. "You know, I had a little bit of a crush on you."

Before he can say anything, the French doors open and Mark appears on the deck, wearing a top hat, which doesn't match his ski parka, and holding a bottle of Winchester scotch.

"People from my childhood!" Mark yells. "Where have you been?"

Jonas looks toward Julia. He wants a glance, an acknowledgment, something, that they will continue their conversation but she is already heading toward her older brother. On the deck she stuffs the pack of cigarettes into Mark's pocket as she takes a gulp of his Winchester.

"Happy New Year, Jonas." Her words are slurred as she goes back into the house with Mark's whiskey. Her face, older and sharper but still delicately etched, burns in him hotter than the bonfire.

"Brat," Mark calls after her, looking at his empty hand, before looking down at Jonas. "Any Straub left down there?"

* * *

The last year Mark had seen Julia, he'd just turned eighteen. He'd stopped by the house to see Mark, who was still at hockey practice. Only Julia was home. All of thirteen, imprisoned by braces and glasses with lenses the size of a periscope, her hair uncombed, Julia stood at the front door and didn't seem willing to let him in.

"What are you doing?" he asked her. He didn't want to go back home, where his own family festered, loud and suffocating. His father molded deep into the recliner, watching Penn State on television in the living room, his mother watching some shopping channel in the den on the smaller portable—what passed in their house for family.

"Why?" She looked as if he might kidnap her, and the ridiculousness of it had made him laugh out loud.

"I'm bored." He shrugged. The house had been quiet, he remembered. It smelled faintly like dust. The floors were hardwood and reflected light. Its sparseness seemed like a truth in some way, one that he hadn't even known existed.

"You can come upstairs." She stood on the bottom step, arms by her side, as he moved toward the sofa. "I was just reading."

In her bedroom he slouched awkwardly into her denim beanbag and leaned over to look through her cassette tapes as she sat on the edge of her bed, bookmarking her paperback.

"This is a good tape." Jonas held up The Cure. "I didn't know you liked them."

"It's Mark's," she answered. "I like it okay. He was getting rid of all his tapes when he bought CDs, so I took them."

"You'll like it better when you're older," he shrugged.

"What does that mean?" She picked up a Care Bear near her pillow and shook it. She then frowned at it before throwing it into the corner, near her dresser.

"I mean you'll have more experiences and stuff, and the songs will mean something."

"I have a life—I'm going roller-skating tonight," she answered. "With Tricia. Ronnie is going to be there."

"So you like Ronnie?" Jonas raised an eyebrow. He tried to remember when he was thirteen, what he thought of girls like Julia back then. Probably nothing, he decided, and that would have been a kindness.

"I just said he was going to be there." She wrapped up all her hair and piled it on her head before letting it fall down onto her shoulders. "That's all."

"What are you going to wear?" he asked, and she gave him that look again. Like he was a perv or something. "I mean, I was just wondering. I always get freaked when I have to figure out what to wear on a date and stuff."

Without speaking, Julia went to her closet and spread the double doors. She pulled a green sweater off the hanger and a pair of dark denim jeans. She laid them out on her bedspread like an empty version of herself. He hopped up and stood beside her.

"That's a great color," he agreed of the sweater. He watched as she took a deep breath, and her proudness made him continue. "It plays well off your eyes."

The door had slammed downstairs, and Jonas took a step toward the hallway. Julia blinked at him, her face pleading without words for him to stay. He could feel her hunger for kindness, for attention. It crackled through his flannel shirt like static. But what more could he say to her about her date with another thirteen-year-old? He heard Mark making his way through the house, equipment banging against the furniture, each bang exploding in his lower spine.

Jonas glanced at the paperback on Julia's dresser. It was Camus' *The Stranger*, and he knew she wouldn't begin to understand that, either, until later. He barely understood it when he was fourteen. Even at eighteen, he didn't feel he had lived enough to really understand anything.

"Hey, have fun roller-skating." He patted her shoulder and stepped out in the hallway, toward Mark.

But maybe she already had understood. Years later, when he was at grad school in Michigan, she wrote him long, angst-filled letters from Berkeley, half-suicidal, cut up over one thing or another. He had wondered in his more panicked moments whether she was depressed or crazy, in and his more reasonable ones, just figuring it all out.

I just want to walk into the bay, she wrote in one letter. *Like that mother in "Interiors."*

You should really watch Ingmar Bergman, not Woody Allen. He had written back.

There was one boy, Patrick, who'd she'd been particularly upset over. They'd dated for a year. One night they had a fight in the lobby of the Castro Theater, which was hosting a Hitchcock film festival. She accused Patrick of being gay, she had explained to Jonas, and Patrick left her in the lobby. She hitchhiked back to Berkeley with a man, she said, who looked like Stephen Stills from Crosby, Stills, and Nash.

I sound like such a whiny creep, she'd written back. *What's wrong with me? I should become a lesbian to get back at him. I watched "Persona" and loved it, by the way—when are you flying out so we can talk hours and hours about it?*

He'd never flown out or seen Julia in person. He'd been dating Karen, who also was working on her Masters at Michigan, and at the time they both thought about staying near the Great Lakes forever. But he'd thought about that day in Julia's bedroom over the years. Something had nagged him about it. He'd been so young himself and had little insight into the nuances of his emotions. He knew, at least, he had felt profoundly sad for some reason.

It wasn't until years later, when Julia began writing him out of the blue, that he'd understood what he'd been feeling was regret. That Julia would one day be smart and beautiful—there has already been hints of it in her soft, curved lips and upturned nose, her long legs, like a colt—and that he might love her. And maybe she might love him. But she was five years younger, and those feelings would never overlap, like sunrise and sunset. At least not until much later. Life suddenly seemed full of endless moments like these, to trip him up, to disappoint him, to complicate his life to paralysis.

After he proposed to Karen, he wrote Julia one last letter. *You should watch 'Wild Strawberries,' it said. And listen to Lloyd Cole. He writes songs for girls like you.* He put the letters she'd written in a box along with his high school ring, a few medals from high school track, a Neil Young pin he'd worn on his denim jacket as a freshman. Things that had mattered, had defined him, once, but not anymore.

* * *

It's after midnight, that he knows, because the fireworks have exploded and the smoke has drifted away, although still faintly on his clothes and he is inside the house, which feels dim, maybe because of the brightness of the exploding cakes, snapdragons, and jumping jacks, or maybe because he is drunk. He moves steadily, careful of his equilibrium, up the stairs and down the hallway to the bathroom. Inside he grips the windowsill with one hand as he pees.

"It's occupied," he says when someone knocks, his voice somewhere around the vicinity of his body as he flushes and scrubs his hands, wets his face. When he opens the door Julia is there, and before he can stop her she pushes him back inside.

"Everyone's still in the yard," she says, as if she can read every one of his thoughts before he can speak them. "Why did you stop writing to me at school?"

"I'm sorry—I proposed to Karen. I had other things on my mind," he answers. He can feel the water still on his face, or is it sweat? He'd been careful not to ask Mark about Julia in the years between the letters and now, only nodding when Mark offered an update on Julia appearing in some cable drama or commercial out in LA, where she worked as an actor.

"I thought we were friends," she says. The bathroom is dark. He reaches over her to turn on the light, but she grabs his wrist.

"We are friends," he says. "But you didn't need my advice. Then or now."

"I didn't want your advice." Her voice is barely a whisper, and the floor of the bathroom suddenly feels like a funhouse underneath his boots. He bends, feeling for the ledge of the tub on his left to sit down and steady himself, but he misjudges and falls in, taking the shower curtain with him, his heading hitting the tiled shower wall.

"Are you okay?" Julia leans forward. But instead of helping him up she kisses him, her breath strong and oily from the whiskey, her tongue quickly searching his mouth. He puts both of his hands on her cheeks and turns his head, gulping the air between them. His head is throbbing from the wall. It feels damp, maybe with blood, maybe sweat.

"Whatever ever happened to Patrick?" he asks. He doesn't know why, but he thinks of him, Julia's boyfriend who left her at the Castro. Julia's letters had kept coming, two or three, after he'd stopped writing, but he'd never even opened them. *Don't encourage her*, Karen had warned him, almost diplomatically, back then, when Karen viewed such things as nuisances and not threats.

But Julia is already standing up, away from him, talking to someone in the doorway. When he looks up, it's Mark. He's still wearing his top hot.

"You okay, buddy?" Mark's expression is somewhere between, as best as Jonas can judge, amusement and concern. "You all right?"

* * *

In the morning, swaddled in bed like he has the flu and not a hangover, Jonas wonders if Julia had been toying with him. He doesn't remember much about last night, except Mark's sweaty body over his in the tub, pulling him up, his top hat falling off and hitting Jonas in the face, like a sad trombone to the evening. He hears voices downstairs—Karen and Mia watching a movie—and wills himself out of bed toward the bedroom closet. He goes through the boxes on the top shelf. The letters from Julia will change nothing, he thinks, even as he sifts through old cassette tapes and letters from friends, other girlfriends, his mother. He remembers the jolt he felt when he'd see Julia's letters in his post office box, her penmanship showy and sometimes urgent, all capped or underlined in the middle of paragraphs. He'd often wondered whether she had wanted to impress him or just someone.

He empties out the last box. The letters are gone. Had Karen gotten rid of them? Had she known him better than himself, that his future self, rattled by some McGuffin, would retrace his steps in the trail to the point where the paths in his life had diverged, looking for answers?

He puts everything away where he found it and calls Mark.

"I think I owe you a new shower curtain," he says. "I'm sorry about last night."

"It's all right, man," Mark coughs. He sounds hoarse. "We were all pretty fucked up."

"How's Julia?" He tries to sound casual.

"Probably as hung over as you, buddy." Marks laughs. "What were you two doing up in that bathroom, man?"

"Didn't Julia tell you?" Jonah asks after a pause. He wonders if they have a story—if hers matches his.

"I'm just kidding, man. She left this morning—made me drive her to the fucking train station so she could see some friends in New York."

When he hangs up, he doesn't know whether he feels sorry for himself or for Julia. It's as if something has been taken away from him, but he doesn't know what it is. Something wonderful and awful at the same time. By the time he'd proposed to Karen, they'd been dating for five years. Although he wasn't sure Karen was the one, he couldn't think of any reasons not to. She was smart and level-headed. Her eyes were like amber, her laugh loud and spontaneous. If someone had had asked him what he'd wanted in a relationship, Karen's composite was his answer. But he hadn't fallen head over heels in love; those electric years of sex and feelings that marked the start of relationships had never ignited for him and certainly wouldn't now. Instead, their relationship grew on him like a spare tire, one that he couldn't work off. He thinks of his father in those later years when he visited him at the cabin in Bedford, looking through a packet of photos from his years in the Navy.

You spend forever, staring at the ocean, waiting to go somewhere, he'd said of trips to China, Southeast Asia, the South Pacific. *But then suddenly you wake up and you've landed, and it ain't that much different from where you left.*

"Find what you were looking for?" Karen asks from the couch when he joins them in the den.

"No." He opens a bottle of water and sinks in next to her. "It probably wasn't important, anyway."

* * *

"Don't tell Mom—not yet, please?" In the passenger seat, Mia burrows her chin into her shirt. Jonas has come to school early—he hadn't meant to, but he'd gotten through his work early and figured he'd sit in the parking lot, listen to NPR, and wait for Mia to get out of swim practice. He'd seen them—Mia and another girl—at the loading dock behind the cafeteria. Mia was standing—although she was facing the dock he recognized her LL Bean parka—and the other girl was sitting on the dock, her legs hooked casually around Mia's legs. Mia held the girl's face in her hands and then began to kiss her.

"I won't." When he turns off the radio, he notices his hand is shaking. "It's our secret."

"Are you mad at me?" She looks at him from underneath the collar of her shirt.

"Why would I be mad?" He turns in his seat toward her.

He's only a little surprised, and only surprised that his suspicions had been correct. Like last summer, when Mia shaved her head. She said it was for swimming, but Jonas wasn't sure. Mostly, he'd thought about thirteen-year-old Julia's room, the posters of Justin Timberlake and ads of shirtless men with Stonehenge stomachs selling perfume. Mia's room had none of those things, only a poster of Rosie the riveter and one of the solar system. In addition to one of Jonas' Lloyd Cole CDs, Mia has downloaded Sleater-Kinney and The Butchies from iTunes. And although incessant texting was something girls did with their friends, Karen and Jonas have yet to meet the girl friend Mia has been obsessively texting.

"I don't know—maybe you wanted something different." Mia stares out the window. Her hair has grown back in some, but she's shaved one half of it again so that one side is whitish-blond peach fuzz, the other spikey and tussled.

"I did want something different," he hears himself say. "But I wouldn't change a thing about you."

"What does that mean?" He feels her looking at him.

"It means." He thinks of Julia. "It means nothing. There are always choices you do and don't make. It just means there's always something you'll be disappointed about in life."

"Her name is Sophie," Mia says after a minute. "I love her, Dad."

He wonders how she's sure. He thinks of telling her she's too young to know. But the realization has been creeping over him for years that he doesn't really know anything. He leans over and kisses her head.

"I'm happy for you." He starts the car. "I hope that, when you're ready, you'll bring her around and introduce us."

***

Karen does the dishes that night, even though it's his job. Later, she joins him in the den, where he plucks the opening notes from Lloyd Cole's "Are You Ready to Be Heartbroken?" on his Stratocaster. It's one of those songs he can't remember all the notes to anymore, but just enough to amble through.

Karen sits on the couch and closes her eyes, her head against the back of the sofa, still holding the dish towel from the kitchen. He puts the Stratocaster down by his chair and joins her.

"I like hearing you play," she says, eyes still closed, as he kneads her shoulders. "It reminds me of Michigan."

"We need to talk." He stops and rests his head on her shoulder. He thinks about the unread letters Julia had sent him. Even if Karen had thrown them away, even if they were gone forever, even if nothing about them would have changed anything, they're important somehow, important evidence in the trajectory of his life. A place marker on the map where the paths in his life began to diverge. He needs to revisit the scene, figure out how he got here. Where he's going next.

"About Mia?" Karen opens her eyes. Of course she thinks he's talking about Mia. She knows everything, or seems to.

"She'll be all right," he answers. Mia's a lot smarter than he was. He hopes. Karen's looking across the room, like something is there, but all Jonas sees is an old concert poster. It suddenly occurs to him he never watched the fireworks at Mark's party; he'd been aware that they were happening, but he was too drunk, too distracted by Julia, too worried about why Mia hadn't texted yet to wish him and Karen a happy new year, and all that was left was smoke curling through the dark.

"Are we?" Karen glances toward him. "Okay?"

"The letters," he says after a minute. "Why did you take them?"

Karen's eye widen as she shakes her head: "What letters?"

* * *

Mia's sleeping; he knows she's not pretending because there's a glistening wet of drool on her pillow, underneath her lips. He sits on the edge of the bed and looks around the darkness; he can barely make out her laptop on her desk, an outgrown stuffed Grover doll on a rocking chair. He wonders where she's keeping his letters. He wonders if she's opened the ones he hadn't, whether they surprised or disappointed her.

And what would he say to her if she asked? That she thinks she's in love now, that she's happy, but that she probably won't stay with Sophie forever? That there would be someone else she'd wind up with, and Sophie would just be that memory that Mia went to, years later, whenever she was unhappy, like an Eden from which she'd been banished?

But he can't keep Mia from heartbreak, from regret. It seems, as a father, a cruelty he hasn't expected. As he gets up to leave, his eyes have adjusted some. He can see Mia's pale, round face, her wide-set eyes, the curl of her fist on her pillow. He can see everything now, as he makes his way to the door, even though they are still in the dark.

SCHEHERAZADE

"Probably just needs a new battery." Dan attaches the claws of his jumper cable to Regina's contacts. "If not that, usually the alternator."

"Should I take it in to the dealer?" She stands near the door of her burgundy-colored Volvo, arms folded like hangers across her thin frame. Dan smiles to himself as he imagines her in this defensive, slightly repulsed posture around children, at sporting events, her students.

"If it doesn't start tomorrow, sure." They've never spoken to each other, even though they've taught their classes in the same building for the last year.

"I can't take it in if it doesn't start tomorrow—that's why I'm asking you whether I should take it tonight."

Her lips purse; even though she's wearing lipstick, all it does is accentuate how lined and frowning they are, how crinkled her eyes, how angular her cheekbones, as if someone stuck a straw in her mouth and tried to suck out her whole fifty-something face.

"I don't know." He shrugs at her tone. She seems the type to turn everything, even a favor, into thinly veiled annoyance. "I guess, if you want to be safe."

Without waiting for her to respond, he climbs into his Jeep and turns on the engine. She watches him steadily, her hands deep in the pockets of her wool coat, chin tucked into her scarf. He sees himself as she does: some mid-thirties jock fuckoff in a North Face parka driving a sport utility vehicle. If that isn't enough to shrivel his balls to the size of skittles, he imagines what one of her students must feel like, her dark eyes piercing into them as they try to explain the differences between the poems of Blake and Wordsworth or whatever it is she teaches in the English department. At least she has tenure, isn't teaching here and at the community college across town, isn't juggling a four-class course load in American History that pays not much more than being a cashier at the grocery store.

She's still standing there, watching him. Through his windshield, he waves her into her Volvo. Then, after a few minutes, he leans out of window.

"Turn it over!" He calls out to her. The car turns but doesn't catch. He holds up his finger out the window, wait, wait, then waves it in a circle, go. This time, it starts.

"You gonna be all right?" He holds the cables and stands by her door as she revs the engine.

"Do you mind following me to the dealership?" Her face has softened. One of her earrings is hooked in the massive waves of curls is that her hair. "It's not far."

Although he's tired, and Karen is already mad at him, he agrees. All his life, he's said yes to things¾baseball, pot, surfing, sex, dirt bikes, road trips, college, LSD. He's not sure where it's all gotten him, except a bunch of crazy stories, but maybe there are a few more "yeses" still that will get him where he needs to be.

* * *

When he wakes up at 5:30, Amy is already awake. As he stumbles outside to meet her, there's still snow in shady corners of the carport, snow that will probably be there for a few more weeks.

"When you get older, it won't be so easy," he says, pulling on his ski cap.

"What, stretching?" She holds up her leg behind her. She's almost as flexible as a gymnast, although she's way too tall—5'8—and too muscular. Her face still has the roundness of youth, though, a shiny, mid-Western creaminess, her hair straight as straw.

"No, getting up," he laughs. He stretches his arms towards the sky and feels the muscles in his back separate. He didn't know at first how he felt about Karen having a daughter. Back then, he didn't know how he felt about Karen, period, only enough to go on another date. To see how things felt after another month. To keep saying yes. Now, five years later, he feels at times that his future has closed on him like the aperture of one of Karen's cameras.

But he stays for Amy. He watches her sprint ahead, her calves pushing against the fabric of her running tights. In a few weeks, softball season will begin. Amy's already got a scholarship from the University of Michigan for the upcoming fall, and to cap off her senior year, she's hoping to take her team to the state finals again. So every morning until the beginning of the season, Dan will wake up at five, run sprints with her, toss her batting practice, and catch hundreds of her fast-pitch softballs before he even has a cup of coffee. When they get home, Amy will shower and Dan will wait for Karen to wake up. He'll stand by the kitchen window and listen for a rustle in the bed, a yawn, a hand on his shoulder, but most times it'll get too late, and he'll wind up going into the bedroom and putting the steaming mug on her night-table, beside her still-sleeping face, and slip out to the university library, grade papers there alone.

***

Just as he passes Regina's office on the way to his own—the one he shares with two other adjuncts—she hurries out, as if she's been waiting for him.

"Here." She holds an envelope, a little bigger than a credit card, out toward him. "I didn't know what to get you."

"For what?" He takes the envelope and peeks inside. It's for the Alley Oop, a burger and beer joint where all the students go to drink and watch games.

"For driving me to the dealer and home." She jerks her hand in the air like it's no big deal. "Just a little thank you."

"Did they find out what was wrong with it? Your car?"

"They're putting in a new battery," she explains. "I'm picking it up tonight."

"Sounds like you're set, then." He wonders where she got the gift card. From the university bookstore? Gone to the restaurant herself?

"If that's what was wrong with it." She smirks. "With my luck, it'll be something worse."

He studies the card again. He knows Amy would love it if they went out to eat, especially to a college place. But the amount on the card is too much in a way he finds slightly insulting—that he had expected something in return for his help.

"You can take your girlfriend, significant other, whoever," Regina adds. She turns to head back to her office.

"How did you get here today?" He looks up. "if you didn't have your car?"

"I got an uber." She gives him that look again, like she's sucking a straw. "I'm not completely helpless."

He laughs. "No, you're sure not."

She stares at the floor between them, and he can see, by the blinking of her eyes, the torrent of thoughts and worry swimming behind them. They're thoughts that bear no relationship to him; he can tell she's already passed him by, like he's a log stuck in the quick-running stream.

Which is where he should leave things, but he wants her to look up at him again, differently, know he is a nice guy, one who helps people and doesn't need to be paid for it.

"I can take you to the dealer," he says suddenly. "You want to eat beforehand? You ever had an Alley Oop burger?"

He expects her to say no, but he at least he can go home, microwave a burrito at Karen's place, and go to sleep with a satisfied conscience.

"I have." The corner of her lip stretches, and it takes him a second to realize she's smiling. "But if you want to waste part of your gift card on me, I'm not going to argue."

* * *

It's crowded at Alley Oop—one of the state's college basketball teams is in the final eight of the NCAA tournament. Dan views this as a positive, as it will mask the awkward silence he assumes will ensue a few minutes after they're seated. They get the only booth in the back, near the bathroom. Regina looks around; it's not disgust, or even bemusement that Dan sees in her expression; she's more pensive than before, even slightly apprehensive. She strokes the table with her index finger, rubbing it in the soft lacquered wood as she holds the laminated oversized menu up with the other.

"So come clean." Dan leans over and smiles. "You come here every Tuesday, don't you?"

"What's Tuesday?" She looks bewildered.

"Twenty-five cent wings," he explains. "It was a joke."

"My daughter went to college here." She picks up the plastic tumbler of water and drinks from it. Even in the din of the restaurant, he can hear her clear her throat. "It's the only place that I remembered after I moved here to teach."

"This place will never die, unless the college does," Dan agrees as the waitress comes to the table. She's about Amy's age and looks at them with a blank smile, as if the disparity in his and Regina's ages and life situations doesn't warrant any reaction or interest. Of course, he probably felt the same way about anyone over twenty-five when he was nineteen or twenty. Back before he understood his own young life was a small, unimportant thing on a very vast ocean.

Dan gets the double cheeseburger, chili cheese fries, and a beer; Regina asks about the soup, the specials, looking at the waitress with an intensity that Dan thinks is probably more reserved for medical board examinations, before deciding on a cheeseburger and diet coke.

"How old is your daughter?" Dan leans back. The banquette is old and he sinks in a little too much, taking him far away from Regina, the table.

"She would have been twenty-eight." Regina's voice is clear, matter of fact, she rolls up her straw wrapper.

Dan takes a long chug of the beer the waitress has put in front of him. He thinks of Amy, listening to music on her phone at home, her softball trophies on the shelf above her bed, the shiny women frozen in the act of swinging or pitching, and the trophies seem so tacky, overkill for such a small, insignificant part of one's life. No trophies, he thinks, of women giving birth, or making tenure. Or standing over a child's casket.

"I'm sorry," he says, wiping his mouth with the back of his hand. "My girlfriend's got a seventeen-year-old."

"They think they know everything at that age," Regina says, again, without inflection, placing the rolled-up straw paper on her napkin.

"Didn't we all?" He smiles. His face is hot—his head, pounding. The bar cheers—someone has slammed dunked, and Dan takes the interruption to let the awkwardness between them slide away, like a droplet of condensation down the side of his beer mug

"You teach history, right?" Regina asks when the bar quiets a little.

He nods. "My father was a history teacher. I figured I'd major in it, since I already knew so much from him."

"Do you have a favorite period?"

"The Civil War. America between the World Wars. The Vietnam War era." He coughs into his fist. "Not because of the wars, but the advancements—scientific and medical—and the cultural upheaval."

"Nothing like a good war to shake things up," she laughs lightly.

"You think that's funny, but it's true." He points at her, smiling. "And it blows kid's minds. What blows your kids' minds?"

"Langston Hughes," she says, sipping her diet Coke.

"Really?" Dan leans over and whispers. "Wow. This college *is* so white."

She smiles at she sips through her straw, her eyes on him. Mission accomplished, he thinks. She no longer thinks he's just some meathead adjunct. And she's easy to talk to, now that her hackles are down. Not overly warm, but pleasant, capable of pleasantries. As they eat, they gossip about some other professors with offices on their hall, Michigan winters, the new parking passes.

But it's still at the back of his mind—the dead daughter. And what about the husband-father? Regina has offered no more personal information, and he's been too afraid to ask.

"Thanks again." She says in his Jeep, her hand on the door latch. They're in the parking lot of the Volvo dealer.

"No problem." He grips the gearshift. "Thanks for dinner. And I, uh, feel really terrible about your daughter. I can't imagine what you've gone through."

She blinks and purses her lips, looking blankly at the door of the glove compartment, and he wonders if he's pushed his luck.

"You shouldn't spend your time worrying about it," she says finally. "Spend your time with her, your girlfriend's daughter."

Before he can answer, she opens the door.

"See you Thursday." She smiles a little smile and then disappears, her coat blowing open as she hurries across the darkened lot.

***

On Tuesday and Thursday evenings, he wears his best sweaters, a splash of cologne. He doesn't have a crush on her or anything, he knows. She's not his type, nor he hers. It's just the novelty of it. Of stopping by Dr. Regina Morgenstein's office and exchanging pleasantries, hearing her laugh and lean back in her chair. Having his colleagues in the history department give him the side eye when he passes. Tonight, when he slows his walk near Office 12B, she's leaning over a telephone book.

"Trouble with the car again?" He pokes her head in her doorway. The office is dim, like always, alit by a single lamp on her desk. He can barely make out the posters of Gertrude Stein, John Dos Passos, on her walls. Every time he stops by, he spends a few seconds studying a corner of her room, a corner of her desk, looking for a photo of her daughter, but hasn't found one. Instead, he has committed to memory the anthologies of American Lit between the Wars that line the shelf to the right of her window, a calendar with students' names written into the boxes of alternating Tuesdays and Thursdays—probably class presentations or office meetings—the mug with a fossilized tea bag in it.

"Oh, no." She shuts the phone book and pats the top of it. "My t—I have a leak. I was just looking for a plumber."

"I can come look at it." He's fixed everything in Karen's house—sinks, roofs, water heaters.

"Oh, that's nice of you, but—"

"But what?" He leans against the doorway.

"It's a toilet." She whispers, leans forward, devouring the entire phone book with her arms and drawing it toward her.

"A toilet?" He says loudly, and she looks up at him, mortified.

"Well, yes, but you don't have to—"

"Your shitter?" He says louder into the hallway, smiling. "You mean something's wrong with your shitter?"

She jaw tightens, and she gives him that look, that one that pulls her features unpleasantly toward the center of her face. But then, like a snapping rope, the tension releases, and she giggles.

"Yes." She nods, touching her neck. "My shitter. So you're coming to come fix it, you said?"

"Maybe you will have a beer in your fridge I can drink for refreshment after my sweaty labor." He winks. "Maybe that beer will be a Guinness."

"Maybe you have a deal." She winks back.

* * *

"She's a colleague of yours or something?" Karen is bent over the developer tray, prodding the white sheet of film. She takes school portraits for a living, covering schools, elementary to high school, over two counties. Her house is littered with contact sheets of children of all ages, skin conditions, and orthodontics, goofy smiles, cowlicks, unflattering eyeglasses. Sometimes he will recognize a 14-year-old girl at the mall or in the parking lot of the high school from her photos stacked on the kitchen table, a circle made with Karen's pen pointing a blemish that she must brush out later with Photoshop.

"She teaches English, not history," he explains. On the wall before them, dripping photos hang of a frozen lake, a snow-covered barn. These are the photos Karen takes on the weekends and during summers when she's not working. Dan tries to guess the picture in the tray before it develops: Owl.

"Her daughter died," he adds, watching the white of the paper begin to fill in with shades of gray.

"Oh, that's sad." Karen taps the center of the photo, and a thicket of trees begins to appear. No owl. "She can't call a plumber?"

"I feel sorry for her, kind of." Dan peers over Karen's shoulder. The darkroom, housed in the half-bath in the basement, is hot and crowded. But he likes the smell of the chemicals, the way Karen pulls her hair back when she's working. He likes watching things develop.

"You going to be gone all Saturday, then?"

"I don't know—why, you have somewhere to be?"

"It's just I might need you for something."

"You can call."

"How old is she?" She nudges him out of the way as he clips the photo to the drying rack.

"Old." He draws out the word. "You know I like older women."

"You better watch it." She pokes him with her tongs. "I'm not that much older than you."

He thinks about Regina, the scowl that appears to be her baseline, the one top incisor that pokes out a little further than the others. The frizzled, dark-reddish hair that doesn't take well to a comb. The way her eyes soften when he pokes his head in her office.

"Just do this one thing for her," Karen says after a minute, like she's giving him permission. "And then you can say no after that."

* * *

He knocks twice before Regina answers. She's wearing dark tights, and oversized sweater. He wonders if she tried on jeans, maybe sweats, before deciding on tights. If she dressed for him. He feels suddenly self-conscious of his waffle Henley and stained sweatpants.

"You look nice," he says to her. "I mean, outside school."

"Oh." Her hand goes to the neck of her sweater. "I—. Thanks."

He feels the back of his own neck burn in embarrassment as he shrugs off his parka, hands it to her without speaking. As she hangs it in the closet, he takes in the living room, the leather chairs and geometric-design rug. A pile of student papers litters the table, along with a half-eaten banana on a napkin. There's photo of a girl, maybe five when taken, on the end table. Her hair is auburn, wild, like Regina's. He steps toward the photo, but Regina's already walking down the hall.

"It's this way." He follows the sound of her voice. The bathroom is bare, unlike his own, where he and Karen and Amy's things fight for space. He bends down and surveys the dripping around the bowl.

"It could be the flange, or the wax ring," he says. "I won't know until I get the toilet off."

"Oh." She crosses her arms in the doorway, frowning. "It sounds like a big job."

"It's really not." He rests back on his haunches. "Parts will run you under $20."

"But how long?" Her tone tightens, like it's his fault the toilet is leaking.

"You have somewhere to be?" He stands up, rubbing his lower back already, before he's even done anything.

"No—no." She holds her hand out for him to stay. "Not until later this afternoon. If it's going to take too long, I'll just call someone."

"How long did you think it was going to take?" He wonders where she's going, and with whom. "Five minutes?"

"No." She shakes her head. "I don't even know. I'm sorry."

He doesn't answer, pulling up the latches of his toolbox. If he'd wanted to get criticized, he thinks, he would have stayed home. When he glances up at her, she wears the same expression the night of the jumpstart, but he understands better it this time: helpless, maybe a little anxious. At the mercy of a stranger. Is he a stranger? He's already helped her twice.

"It's okay," he says after a minute. "It really won't take long. Unless it's a big repair—you'd need someone else at that point. But I can fix a flange or a wax ring."

"It's just—I don't want to get ripped off," she says, trailing her fingertips on the countertop. "When the roofers came last year—"

"You won't get ripped off," he says. "I won't let you. Okay?"

"Okay." She nods, taking a step out of the doorway. "Do you want some coffee or something?"

"I'll hold out for the Guinness," he says. After she leaves he works quickly, shutting off the water valve and loosening the bolts from the tank. He listens to Regina move around the house—the clanking of a teacup, the groan of a floorboard. But mostly it's quiet. When he steps into the living room fifteen minutes later, she jumps out of her armchair, sliding a bookmark into a book.

"Don't get up." He wipes his hands on his pants. "I gotta run out and pick up a wax ring."

"I should go with you." She puts the book on the coffee table. "To pay."

"It's just the hardware store." He shrugs, glancing at the cover. Something about Early Romantic poets. "Not the opera."

"I've been to a hardware store," she says, fetching their coats from the closet. "Have you been to the opera?"

"You inviting me?" He jokes. She pauses, holding his parka, before extending it out to him.

"Do you like opera?" she finally asks.

"I don't know." He probably doesn't. But he would say yes, of course, if she asks him to go. "Maybe."

"I'll keep that in mind." She turns to the door. "Shall we go?"

At first he thinks she means the opera, but then he realizes she means the hardware store. Still, he allows himself this little fantasy on the drive over: the tux he'd probably have to rent, or maybe he could get away with the suit he wears to weddings. What would Regina wear? She doesn't have much of a figure: rail thin and lacking in all the important proportions. However, it's delicate, feminine and, like a clothing store mannequin, looks good in everything. Would they have dinner first? Italian? Something more daring?

At the last minute of his fantasy, he inserts Karen in place of Regina. Karen would find opera too long, too boring, be more interested in critiquing what everyone was wearing and how unflattering it made them look. Maybe, he thinks, the measure of enthusiasm for something is proportional to the person you're sharing it with.

At the store, he watches Regina run her hand lightly over items on the shelves—toilet flappers and packaged fill valves—as if trying to decipher Braille. He imagines running his own hand, over her forehead, her heart.

"I've been teaching Amy—my girlfriend's daughter—how to change her oil," he explains in line. "So she doesn't have to ask a lunkhead like me to do it. It seems hard, stuff like this, but it's easy to learn, and you feel kind of like, I don't know—empowered. Like you've got a handle on your shit."

"Do you feel like you've got a handle on your 'shit'?" Regina smiles lightly. "I'm not being facetious, I just was wondering."

"I just need to get Amy off to college and then, I don't know." He shrugs, glancing at the shelf of screwdrivers with orange handles that are displayed along with duct tape and other last-minute pickups above the conveyer belt. He likes orange, likes the bold colors in the hardware store because they seem so sure of themselves. That and everything is measured—to solve the problem, you only need the correct-size bolt or ring or nail.

"Don't know what?" she presses.

"Anything. Nothing." He shrugs. He doesn't want to talk about Karen, not when she's not here to defend herself. And he wouldn't know how to explain it anyway, except everyone already knows the gist of how it feels: that you've grown apart, or that you were never quite that close to begin with. On the same airplane, going the same general place, but different destinations once it lands.

He's screwing the tank back into the bathroom tile when he hears a knock at Regina's door. He makes an extra clang with the tank as footsteps, heavy, creak into the living room. Voices, male laughter, Regina's laughter. He's finished and slowly puts his tools away, wiping the sweat off his brow as it dawns on him that he will have to leave the house in front of this man, whoever he is, boyfriend or whoever who can't even fix a fucking toilet.

"My colleague" is how Regina introduces Dan to John. John's bespectacled and bearded, sweater-vested, with a surprising amount of sandy, layered hair. A firm handshake. The kind of guy who probably goes to the opera.

"Weekend plumber." Dan jokes, going toward the closet for his parka. He wonders how Regina and John met. What she sees in him. "You kids have a fun evening planned?"

"Just dinner." The man holds his trench coat folded over his arm. "And a movie."

"I owe *you* dinner," Regina says to Dan, stepping toward him, reaching to touch his arm. "I'm so grateful."

"Nope¾we're even," Dan jokes, stepping away, his wool cap and parka on. He holds up the six-pack of Guinness Regina has left by the door. "You already bought me dinner once. People are going to talk."

***

The sun is out longer now, another hour than before, the air not quite so frigid. On the mound, Amy winds up and he braces, squatting behind home plate. He doesn't think as much as reacts. Closes his glove tight when he feels the pop of the ball in it. Then he stands, tosses it back, and waits for her to fire it at him again.

"Looking good," he says after the fiftieth pitch. "Just make sure you're keeping your power foot straight, okay? You're falling off to the side a little."

His phone vibrates, and he digs it out of his pocket as Amy gathers stray softballs.

"Is this a bad time?" It's Regina. Her voice, disembodied from her, takes him by surprise. It's soft and crisp around the edges, lighter and sweeter than the lips from which it comes.

"No." He steps back toward the batting cage. "Is something wrong with the toilet?"

"Oh, no," she laughs. "It's perfect. But I just...felt bad about Saturday. How things ended."

"What do you mean?" But he thinks he knows what she means. The way he went home in a bad mood, emptied two cans of Guinness sitting on the couch before halftime of the Wolverines game.

"Transactional. I should have canceled on John…"

"Why?" He picks a softball near his sneaker. "It was perfect timing for you."

"What are you doing tomorrow? Do you eat breakfast?"

"Why are you asking?"

"Will you come over? Homemade waffles? For your trouble?"

He counts to three before saying yes. He knows, at some point, he will have to say no. Before it's just something else for Karen to find fault with. Like his poker nights, or his fantasy league. But for now, he is riding the crest of a wave, waiting to see where it ends, whether he can tack away without wiping out.

"Who was that?" Amy is close to him now, the canvas knapsack of softballs slung over her shoulder.

"One of my colleagues." He stuffs the last softball in her knapsack.

"You go to your colleagues' houses for breakfast?" She cocks an eyebrow. Amy knows the pulse between Dan and her mother is weak. But they don't speak of it much, afraid to upset their own delicate balance.

"When they want to make it for me," Dan grins, then adds without prompting. "She's a little older than your mother… and her daughter died."

"Oh." Amy exhales heavy, through her nose. "I guess that's nice of you, then."

"That's all it is." He touches her shoulder. "You shouldn't worry."

"It's just." She frowns, eyes, upward, in frustration, before looking at him. "I mean, I worry about you and Mom sometimes."

"Don't worry about stuff like that." Dan eases the knapsack off her shoulder. He remembers when she weighed about the same as it. "Worry about your power foot."

***

"I haven't made waffles in years," Regina says as she puts the plate in front of Dan. She hurries back to the kitchen and returns with whipped cream and sliced strawberries. "I'm happy if I get a good cup of coffee before I start working."

"Me, too—although Amy was giving me a hard time about not making her breakfast the other day," Dan says, spreading his napkin across his lap. "Like I don't get before dawn every morning to run with her, practice with her, go to all her games."

"You like being a father," Regina says, more of a statement than a question. She studies him over the table. She's doing that thing again with her finger, he notices, rubbing it against the tablemat, and he pauses before answering. He thinks about the curly haired girl in the picture, if he should talk about Amy at all.

"Yeah, I do." He stares at his waffle. "I mean, I would have been a father-father, too, but Karen doesn't want any more kids."

"Does that bother you?"

"I haven't thought much about it—I mean, one is a handful. Amy's a good kid, though—really smart and never gets into any trouble."

"Amy's a lucky girl." Regina smiles over her coffee. "Her mother, too."

"*I'm* lucky," Dan quickly, biting into his waffle, feeling the back of his neck tingle. "Wow, these are amazing. If I made waffles this good, I'd make them every day."

"Hmm." Regina holds up her fork, mouth full. "You know, I haven't made them since...well, since Kate was a teenager."

"How long...has she been gone?" Dan lays his fork against his plate.

"Five years," she answers. Both of her hands tug at the ends of her napkin, the middle taut.

"I'm sorry." He doesn't know what to say, what she would want to hear.

"Sorry won't bring her back." She stares at her coffee mug. "I'd prefer you not say it."

"Yeah, okay." He nods, and he's feels stupid, like he's failed a test.

"I shouldn't have said that." She puts her hand on the table, toward his. "I'm sorry. I shouldn't have even told you. I don't want you to pity me."

"Does John know about Kate?"

"Of course." She draws her hand back, tucking it under the table. "But that's different."

"Different how?"

"I mean, I didn't want you to be here for that." She wipes some crumbs off the table into her hidden palm. "Because you pity me. That's why you keep coming, right? Because of Kate and because you think I can't do anything and because you feel sorry for me."

"No," he says. "That's not why."

"Then why?"

"Because I have a theory about saying yes to everything," he explains. "And I've said yes some crazy things."

"Well, now I have to know what," she smiles.

"I'll tell you just one," he says. "When I was in college, one semester I worked at this turkey farm east of Lansing as a turkey calmer."

"So you—"

"Exactly," Dan laughs. "Chickens are easy to slaughter, because they're kind of stupid, but turkeys are whip smart. So they knew what was going down and freaked the fuck out, fought back. So my job was to talk to them, calm them down, help them cross that bridge of acceptance."

"That actually worked, the talking?" She leans back in her chair, wide eyed, mug in both hands. "What did you say?"

"Believe it or not, yes, it worked. I just told made up epic stories about their lives, or the magnificent turkey retirement home to which they were headed."

"Tell me one story." She raises her eyebrows. "Please."

"There was this turkey¾big wattle and a long snood. Really big body. I mean, he was the Tom Brady of turkeys. So that was what we called him, Tom. I told him he was the Greatest of All Turkeys, that he'd won so many Super Bowls not only was the President going to pardon him but that he was going to start for the Patriots on Thanksgiving."

"And then?"

Dan draws his finger across his neck. "Felt so bad. If there was one I could've saved, it would've been him."

"You can't save anyone," she says quietly, like she's not speaking to him.

"I never repeated the same story twice," he says, pretending he hasn't heard. "It was like, I don't know, *Arabian Nights*, but for turkeys."

"Scheherazade," she laughs. "It fits you."

"Turkey Scheherazade," he corrects.

* * *

Even though he should leave, she makes him another waffle, another cup of coffee. In the living room, he flips through a pile of student papers on the coffee table while he waits for her to brush her teeth, so they can walk out together. Papers about the poems of Yeats. A set-off couplet in one of the pages catches his eye: *But one man loved the pilgrim soul in you/And loved the sorrows of your changing face.*

Yeats does not mean Thanksgiving pilgrim, the student of this particular essay has written of the couplet. *Because there is no Thanksgiving in Ireland.*

"In case we don't do this again," Regina says at the front door. "And I guess there's no reason to, I wanted you to hear it from me, and not anyone else."

"Hear what?"

"Kate, she killed herself."

Her words are so unexpected that his response, "Oh," falls out of his mouth with the heft of a boulder. It craters between them as Regina steps onto the porch, pulling her scarf tight around her neck with her free hand.

"It's locked," she says, as if she hasn't heard him, adjusting the strap of her briefcase, jigging her keys. She nods at the doorknob. "Just close it behind you."

***

"Are you happy?" He asks Amy, who's lying on the other side of the couch. They're watching TV, waiting for Karen to come home from a late night at work. .

"Yeah." She texts something on her phone before looking at him. "Why?"

"Just asking." He digs in the bag of Doritos and feels nothing but waxy bag and crumbs. "You know, kids are good at hiding stuff."

"I'm got a scholarship to Michigan. I'm graduating this spring." Amy opens her mouth wide. "And I got my braces off, finally."

"Yeah, you're the bomb." He grins, wiping his greasy hand on his sweatshirt. "Seriously, though, when you and Jeff broke up—are you over him?"

"That was last fall—he's so stupid." Amy piles her hair atop her head. It looks like silver queen corn. People think he and Amy are siblings. "Why are you asking all of the sudden?"

"I read some article on teen suicide," he lies. "And the signs—sometimes they're subtle. Or, you know, sometimes things seem like the end of the world because you're a teenager and you've never experienced them before, when the reality is that, in ten years, Jeff won't mean squat to you."

"He don't mean squat to me now." Amy reaches for the empty bag. "You didn't leave me any Doritos?"

"We have another bag." He hops up and goes into the kitchen. The girl he dated in college, Julia, she was the one who messed his shit up. Breaking up with him before graduation, after they'd agreed to drive around Canada for a few weeks, visit some distant family of his east of Vancouver. After he'd applied to grad schools in Illinois so he could be close to her while she attended the law school at University of Chicago. After he'd already fallen in love with her, planned to marry her, father their children. It still meant squat to him, a little bit, when he was mad at Karen or drunk or just couldn't sleep at night and scrolled through her photos on Facebook, her two children, her lawyer husband. His heart had been Hulk-smashed, and even though he put it together, it was a vase with a piece missing, one that he was supposed to display proudly on his coffee table, anyway.

"I'll miss you when I'm at school," Amy says when Dan comes back with the party-size bag he'd talked Karen into getting last Saturday at the grocery store.

"I won't be that far away." He settles on the couch, drawing her legs atop his. He opens the bag with a pop and hands it to her. "You can always come home on the weekend, but you'll have so many friends, then, you totally won't want to hang out with your mother's boyfriend."

They're both quiet. Maybe they're wondering whether he'll still be Karen's boyfriend then. There was a trial period, last year, when they decided, at Karen's suggestion, to live apart for a while. Dan stayed at his mother's house, where he fixed the dryer and cleaned the shutters and watched *The Golden Girls* reruns somewhat un-ironically while eating tuna casserole, wondering if he finally should go to grad school. But then Karen broke her leg skiing, asked him to come back. Dan, in the choose-your-own-adventure of his life, said yes.

After Amy goes upstairs, Dan fetches his cell phone and sits on the deck. He cracks open a beer and watches his breath cloud the air before calling.

"I'm sorry—it's late, but—could I ask you something?"

"Um, sure, I guess." Regina sounds sleepy. He hears shuffling in the background, thinks maybe she's sitting up in bed. He wonders if John is with her.

"I'm really sorry—I shouldn't have called."

"But you did. So ask."

"I don't want this to come off as insensitive or whatever, but do you know...why she did it? Kate?"

There is a long silence, marked by Regina's breathing, and he concentrates on the cold beer can burning his palm as he waits for her to hang up on him.

"She didn't leave a note," she says finally. "I really don't know of a specific reason."

"Do you hate me? I'm sorry."

"Why would I hate you?"

"For asking. It's just...I don't know. For her to feel so helpless, so unhappy. It made me start worrying about Amy."

"Is she having problems?"

"No, no—nothing like that." He pauses and takes a sip of beer. "She got dumped last fall, but she seems to have gotten over it. She must think I'm insane for asking."

"I'm glad you asked her. You just never know."

"And people are different, you know? When my college girlfriend and I broke up, for a long time I felt pretty hopeless, though I didn't tell anyone."

"What did you do?"

"I was supposed to start grad school, but I moved to San Diego with a few buddies instead. Taught myself to surf. Surfed every day I could. I literally drowned myself," he laughs. "Well, not literally. But it made me—my feelings—kind of insignificant, I don't know, a broke and broken kid in this vast ocean. And I waited tables and read biographies of American presidents and slept in a sleeping bag on the floor. But mostly I surfed."

"You came back, though—to Michigan?"

"When my father died. My sister had gotten married and lived too far away, and, I don't know, I didn't want my mom to be alone."

"Do you ever think about going back?"

"To San Diego?" He has. Secretly, only when he is alone, as if afraid his own thoughts would betray him. But what would he do there? He's thirty-two, ten pounds heavier, an adjunct without a PhD, who needs to sleep on a mattress these days. "Nah. Do you ever think of going back?"

"Where?"

"Wherever you were before you came here."

"New Jersey? No, I don't think I'll go back there."

"I'm really sorry for waking you."

"It's okay," she says, and he hears moving around again, the hum of the microwave. "I have a hard time sleeping."

"Me too." He leans back in the deck chair. "I have this weird panic, like I should have figured out what to do by now and I keep waiting for that sign, being open to it."

"To saying yes to everything."

"Right," he laughs. "You remembered."

He hears the sliding door open behind him and tenses.

"Who are you on the phone with?" He feels Karen's voice, like a burn all over his shoulders.

"My colleague," he says, sitting up straight.

"It's late. Come to bed." With that, the door slides shut behind him.

"Are you in trouble?" Regina's voice sounds light, bemused.

"Nah—she gives me shit for everything," he whispers. "And the funny thing is, it doesn't matter what—I could leave crumbs on the counter or have an affair—both are like DEFCON 1."

"Well, all things being equal, you should have the affair, then."

"I don't want to." Still, he feels like Regina has overturned a bucket of ice water in his stomach. "I mean, I would want something more than that. Like, someone I could talk to. About anything. That's all."

"Still, you should go," she says. "Before DEFCON 1."

"Hey, I'm sorry I woke you, Regina, and made it all about me."

"You didn't. I'm happy you called, Dan. See you tomorrow?"

He doesn't go to bed right away. Instead, he puts his cell on the table inside, in a show of good faith if Karen comes back downstairs, and returns to the deck with his half-empty beer. He thinks about surfing—how he bought a used longboard for two hundred bucks with his graduation money and just paddled out in the cold water, figuring it out as he went along. You could be lost in an ocean, but there was potential. A sliver of coastline popping up over the horizon, an open harbor. A boat. A plane. It was the other way, being on dry land, finding it inhospitable, and knowing how long it took you to get there in the first place, that scares the hell out of him.

* * *

When Amy pitches, it's a thing of beauty. Her right arm rises, like the minute hand of a clock, up to twelve. In unison, her right leg drives down and forward as her arm falls, before switching to her left foot, lifting it, her arm now at four o'clock, then eleven, making a complete rotation with her arm while driving her right foot toward her left, before releasing the ball underhanded at the six o'clock position. Dan has watched this controlled chaos for hours, in slow-motion on videotape, in real life in the mornings, and it amazes him each time, the way she hurls herself out into space over and over. She's like a giant heart and its ventricles, contracting, expanding, pushing out blood, oxygen.

"Did you lock the car?" Karen asks beside him in the stands.

"Uh-huh." He doesn't take his eyes from Amy as she bends over the mound, ball in glove, waving off a sign. "Why?"

"I don't remember it clicking. Are you sure?" There is a precedent for Karen's paranoia. Late for a shoot last year, she'd forgotten to lock the doors of her Windstar in the parking lot of a neighboring high school and returned at the end of the day to find several hundred dollars of supplies stolen.

"Do you want me to go back there and check?"

"Would you?"

He sighs and climbs down the stands, through the concourse, and into the parking lot. There's nothing in his Jeep, and it's on him if it gets broken into, anyway, but he knows if he doesn't do it, it will escalate. It's not about the Jeep, or whether he locked the door at home or put his clothes in the hamper. It's about being in control, something, since Karen's ex-husband cheated on her, she's had trouble feeling.

Plus, Karen's actually speaking to him, ending the three days of radio silence that followed after she came home and found him on the deck, talking to Regina on the phone.

At his Jeep, he sits in the driver's seat with the door open and digs out a pack of cigarettes from the side door. Karen wasn't always this way, and early on, he'd always written off her paranoia, her mood swings, and controlling behavior to stress, a bad day, a one-off. But it's been five years, and the realization that it will never stop drives Dan to furtively smoke cigarettes on the way to school, or times like these, when he can't be sure which way the wind will blow, whether Karen will be satisfied with the locked car door and the day will resume without incident or whether it will be a precursor to something larger.

He's halfway through the cigarette when his phone rings.

"Where are you?" Karen asks, sounding annoyed.

"I had to stop in the bathroom," he lies, holding the cigarette away from his phone, as if she can see it and smell it.

"You're not lying, are you?" She doesn't mention what he's lying about, but he wonders if it's Regina. He's deliberately avoided her this week, rolling into the arts building at school at the last minute and hanging out in the men's room after class. Part of it's Karen, but part of it's maybe to see if Regina will forget about him, if she will retreat back into her world of early Romantic poets and Constant Comment tea and sweater vest John and he can tell himself that he was being stupid, getting all worked up about her, someone he has no business getting worked up about in the first place.

"No, I'm not lying to you," he says to Karen, digging around in his change holder for his breath mints. "Should I bring you back some toilet paper as proof?"

"Will you bring me a pretzel?"

At the concessions stand, discovering there are no pretzels, he buys both himself and Karen hot dogs, a big Diet Coke. As he heads over to the condiments bar, his phone rings again. He's about to throw it onto the concrete when he sees it's Regina. He holds it like it's the timer on a bomb. There's no way to erase the record of her calling, if Karen happens to go through his phone. But he doesn't have to answer.

Still, his stomach feels fluttery, his head light. The ringing stops, and after a few seconds his phone vibrates, indicating a new voicemail.

"I'm sorry to call you during the weekend." Regina's voice envelopes his ear. "I just—I guess I'm being paranoid. I worry I said something wrong, which is entirely possible, knowing me. Anyway, you don't have to call back. I'm sure I'll see you around at school. I hope you're doing well—I'm sure you are—bye."

He replays it three, four times, memorizing the cadence of her voice, the pauses, the sound of her breaths, and when the phone rings again he nearly squirts mustard from the dispenser onto his wrist instead of the hot dog and this time and yes, he will answer it, but it's Karen, not Regina.

"Amy's batting next," she says. "Hurry up—you're going to miss her."

*　*　*

When he gets to campus and sees Regina's car in the second row, he brakes and backs up. He should have just gone to the other lot, where he parked all last week, but he realizes it's gone too far now, that it looks like he's avoiding her. Besides, he thinks as he taps the gas and glides into a spot one row over, she's not stupid. She'll know what to say, what not to say. How to gracefully churn out mindless pleasantries in passing for the next few weeks until the semester finishes and they have the whole summer to figure out how never to see each other ever again.

"Hey." In the arts building, he knocks on the doorframe of her office. "How's kicks?"

"Kicks are fine," she answers, not looking up from her laptop. "Kicks good for you, too?"

She plays the part even more perfectly than he could have imagined. And yet it just makes him feel worse. When he doesn't answer, she looks up at him. The corners of her lips are screwed tight into her face, like he's just told her he doesn't have his paper to turn in because his Internet wasn't working.

"I'm sorry I haven't been around much," he says finally. "it's just—"

"DEFCON 1?" She raises her eyebrows.

"You want to go to a movie? Like right now?" He steps inside and closes her door. "Or dinner? We can leave notes in our classrooms saying we had emergencies."

"Before finals week?" She laughs. "My students would hunt me down in the theater."

"Not if we saw that Swedish film at the Independent," he says. "Subtitles are undergrad repellant."

"What would Karen say?" Regina leans back in her chair, looking at him mischievously.

"What would John say?" He gives her the look back.

"Well, at least I know you would say yes." She closes her laptop and opens her drawer. "But can we take a raincheck?"

"What's that?" He notices a pile of plastic cards in the drawer with a rubber band around them. He wonders if this is where his Alley Oop gift card came from, if she has a bunch lying around to give out to anyone when situations arise, and he feels big and dumb and stupid.

"These?" She holds them up. "They're gift cards I bought for my daughter to use. Not all at once—some were for college, some for birthdays, holidays. I didn't realize she hadn't used any of them until after she was gone. Anyway, a bunch are expired, but some aren't. Do you want them?"

She spreads a few on the desk—Bath & Body Works, the Gap, Wayfair.

"I wish I had actually bought her things." She picks up a card. "But I didn't know what she liked anymore. I thought I was doing her a favor, but maybe she felt I couldn't be bothered."

"I'm sure she appreciated it." Dan's eyes fall on Regina's shoulders. They slump inward as she stares intently at the card, eyes unblinking. He wonders if she's going to cry. What he would do if she did.

"I have an idea." He leans over and picks up a few of the gift cards. "For our rain check."

* * *

"You bought all this stuff yourself?" Karen looks at the shower gift basket from Bath & Body Works, the comforter and sheet set from Bed Bath & Beyond, the new cleats from Dicks.

"Just some graduation/going-away gifts for Amy," Dan explains as he packs everything in a Rubbermaid container to hide in the garage. He doesn't mention that he went to the mall with Regina, that they spent an hour at Bath & Body Works spraying fragrances onto little paper slithers and also on their wrists, cherry blossom and wisteria and wild blueberry vanilla, interrogating the sales staff as to what scents high school girls liked. *It's for our daughter*, Dan had explained, joking, and realizing its potential poor taste, turned to Regina apologetically. But instead of castrating him with that look of hers, she reached over and squeezed his hand. Her fingers were warm, almost feverish, curled over his, and he froze, not wanting her to let go, but maybe she mistook his stillness for embarrassment or mild revulsion and moved her hands quickly to a candle, bringing it up to her face.

"Did you hear what I just said?" Karen's hand is on the side of his cheek and he recoils, wondering if she's going to smack him or something for zoning out.

Instead, she caresses it. "I said that was really nice of you, doing this for Amy. She's going to love it. And all this time I thought you hated the mall."

* * *

It's late at night, after eleven, when Dan gets to Regina's house. She'd called him in tears, mumbling incoherently about John.

I'm missing a student paper, Dan had said to Karen, pulling on his coat and grabbing his keys. *I must have left it in the office. I'll be back soon.*

Regina's wearing a dark plum dress, pantyhose, when she opens the door. "I shouldn't have called you." She shakes her head. "I don't even know why I called you."

"What happened?" He steps over the threshold of the door. Regina's shoes rest at odd angles behind her, as if she kicked them off mid-walk.

"John and I broke up."

Dan hangs his coat in the closet, giving himself a minute to process what she's told him. He thinks of an island, once a dot over the horizon, easily mistaken for detritus, now visible.

"You want some wine?" When he turns, she has already poured herself a glass. Or another one.

"I have to get up early." He waves her off. "So, who broke up with who?"

"I broke up with him." She flops down onto the couch, wine spilling over the rim of her glass. "John is insecure, prone to bouts of extreme jealousy, and misguided possessiveness."

"Huh. He sounds nice." Dan recorks the bottle resting on the table.

"Oh, he is, he was, most of the time." She takes a long sip. "Until I met you."

"You told him he had nothing to worry about?" He sits across from her. He crosses his legs, tries to look relaxed. But he feels ready to explode out of himself. A vein throbs in his ankle, his neck. "You told him I was gay, right?"

She leans over, hand on her stomach, and laughs. When she looks at him, her mascara has started to run a little.

"That's what I like about you." She dabs the corner of her eye with her pinky. "You always make me laugh."

"Seriously, if he's a jealous type, you don't need that in your life," he says. "And I could've told you this over the phone."

"Did I get you in trouble again, speaking of jealous types?" She bends over, like a clam shell. From within that shell he can hear her voice, very small. "I'm sorry."

"It's okay." He stands up. "But I don't want to fight about who has the more possessive partner."

"If you don't like her—Karen." Regina looks up. "Why don't you just leave? Amy—I know, Amy. But she's graduating in a few months. You can always stay in touch with Amy."

"I thought we were talking about you and John." He shoves his hands in his pockets as she leans back against the couch, drawing her knees in with her arms. She looks like a little bird, all tucked into herself, and he imagines lifting her up and cradling her, talking to her like one of those turkeys.

"We were. Now we're talking about you." She pokes her head up. "You talk about saying yes to people, Dan. You need to say yes to yourself."

"What do you mean?"

"What do you want?" She closes her eyes, her head against the sofa cushion. "What do you want?"

With that, she's quiet. He wonders if she's passed out. He goes over and gently slides his arms under her legs, her back. Then he carries her to the bedroom. When he places her in the middle of the bed, she tightens her arm around the back of his neck and opens her eyes. Without saying anything, he lowers himself on top of her.

***

When he hears his cell phone vibrating, he knows it's not the first call Karen's made. All throughout his dreams, he heard something buzzing, didn't know what it was. He reaches over and grabs it from the night table, looking at the caller ID.

"Dan." He hears Regina turn over, shake his arm. "You should probably answer that."

"And say what?" He closes his eyes, lets himself remember what happened the night before. That it wasn't horrible, as he feared it would be. That he liked it. That he would do it again. He opens his eyes and turns to her. She sighs and runs her fingers through his hair. He can see the beginning of stubble in her armpits, a mole the size of a pin above her right breast.

"Whatever you need to tell her has nothing to do with this," she says. "This can't happen again."

"Why?" He's so surprised he's unable to hide his disappointment.

"Because." She shakes her head. "You're in a relationship. And we're at such different places in our lives."

"You knew that last night, before you broke up with John." He sits up, feeling around under the sheets for his boxer shorts. "Before you called me."

"I did, but I was drunk."

"That makes me feel so much better." He fingers what appears to be Regina's bra and hands it to her.

"I didn't mean it like that." She squeezes his arm. "I meant there are things that you might want but have no practical way of existing."

"They can." He stares at his phone, vibrating again. "All you have to do¾"

"Is say yes?" she answers, smirking. And then, after a minute, as if in apology: "It's funny, if Kate had brought you home, I would have thought she'd lost her mind. But after getting to know you, I would've been so happy for her. Of course, she would have never dated someone like you—she was so angry at the world most of the time."

She stops speaking, her shoulders heaving, her body slouching in waves, like a rockslide on a mountain.

"I worry that it's my fault—the anger. I worry she got it from me. I worry I'm a bad person. A broken person. I worry that it's my fault she killed herself."

She screws her eyes shut and waits for the wave of grief to pass over before continuing. "And I'm not—trying to live her life for her. I just, naturally, since you're not much older, I often think about where she would be in her life in the context of yours—would she be in her career? Would she be happy? Would she be happy in her relationship? I'm sorry—you are just full of life. I find myself comparing."

He leans over and draws her into his arms. They rock back and forth, like they're on a boat. Out here, he thinks, in the water, everyone is lost.

* * *

"I looked up her." He hears Karen say through the deadbolted door. "Dr. Morgenstein. And when I drove by her house last night, guess who's Jeep was parked out front at three in the morning? I thought you just had to get a file off your work computer, Dan, huh! Isn't that what you said? You goddamn liar!"

"I don't know what to say." He looks back at the driveway, at his luggage, his PlayStation, his aftershave can scattered about the lawn. "Except I'm sorry."

"What about Amy?!" He sees Karen's bloodshot eyeball through the crack before she slams it again. "You were her world!"

He packs everything on the lawn into his Jeep. He could probably crash at his mother's again, until he figures out his living arrangement. When he left Regina's, they'd agreed to talk once he'd figured out his situation with Karen. She'd kissed his cheek and pressed a travel mug of coffee into his hand. He'd been too sick to his stomach to even drink it. He drives to the high school and waits in the parking lot until the afternoon classes let out. Then, when he sees Amy, jumps out of the car.

"I'm sorry." He walks along the sidewalk toward. Amy's lip is parted, the hinge of her jaw loose and hanging. She juts her head down, pulling her backpack close to her. "You lied to me," Amy says when they get to her Ford Escort. "You lied about that woman."

"I wasn't," he answers. "At the time, I wasn't."

"Just leave me alone." She slides into the driver's seat.

"So, that's it—after everything we've done together?" He folds his arms. Of course she would side with Karen. But he had hoped that maybe she wouldn't.

"It doesn't mean you can cheat on us." She slams the door but doesn't start the engine.

"Amy, I love you." He puts his palms on the glass. "Nothing will change that."

She cracks the window. "Do you love my mom?" He understands if he says yes that Amy can talk to Karen, that forgiveness can happen, that things maybe would be okay.

But for some reason, he thinks about all those school portraits lying around Karen's, all the years of pimples, braces, awkwardness. All those kids trapped forever in their least-liked versions of themselves. "No," he says. "I don't. I'm sorry."

Back at his Jeep, he squeezes in among the boxes, the clothes and stereo equipment, his dumbbells. In the rearview mirror he sees the Tupperware container of gifts in back seat. Should he have left them at the house, let Karen give them to Amy? Would she even have done that, or would she have thrown them away? Would they now sit in the corner of his office, like a bunch of unused gift cards?

He closes his eyes, just for a minute, before he has to think about what happens next. He imagines Tom Turkey, if he were still here, nestled somehow comfortably atop the CD rack, his talons scratching up Van Halen to The Who all the way to Wilco, in the passenger seat.

"I'm sorry, man, for lying to you guys like that," Dan would say to him. "It was a shitty thing to do."

"It's all right, guy," Tom would answer. "It wasn't lying, exactly. You were just telling us what we wanted to hear. It was the thought that counted."

"Speaking of which, tell me I'll be all right," Dan says aloud.

When Tom answers, Dan already knows the tale. He knows how it ends. Of course he does. And there are some bad parts, but there are good parts, too. He sips the coffee, long cold, and waits to hear the good parts.

Jen Michalski is the author of three novels, three short story collections, and a couplet of novellas. Her latest novel, *You'll Be Fine*, was a 2021 Buzzfeed "Best Small Press Book," a 2022 Next Generation Indie Book Awards Finalist, and was selected as one of the "Best Books We Read This Year" by the Independent Press Review. She's the editor of the weekly online literary weekly *jmww* and currently lives in Southern California, although she will always be a Baltimore girl by heart. Visit her at jenmichalski.com